THE PLAIN BRIDE

CHASITY BOWLIN

ALSO BY CHASITY BOWLIN

THE DARK REGENCY SERIES

The Haunting of a Duke

The Redemption of a Rogue

The Enticement of an Earl

A Love So Dark

A Passion So Strong

A Heart So Wicked

An Affair So Destined

STANDALONE

The Beast of Bath

Worth The Wait

THE DUNNE FAMILY SERIES

The Last Offer

The First Proposal

The Other Wife

The Late Husband

The Plain Bride (coming soon)

The Perfect Groom (coming soon)

THE LOST LORDS SERIES

The Lost Lord of Castle Black

PROLOGUE

1814

SINCLAIR WORTHAM, Lord Mayville, entered the library that was his father's sanctuary and sank down onto the chair that faced the desk. It was habit, he supposed, to sit on that side of the desk. He couldn't bring himself to take his father's seat. It wasn't respect; it wasn't even grief. Lingering disgust would be a better description.

In the days since his father's untimely death, so many horrific things had come to light that he couldn't quite take them all in. Everything he'd thought he knew about their family, about their history, had been a lie. His father and his grandfather before him had been monsters. Traitors. Men who had traded their loyalty to king and country to the highest bidder. Their fortunes, the palatial homes and estates that had been passed through generations, had been paid for with the blood and grief of countless English families. How many people had died, how many people had grieved, as a result of their misdeeds? His own brother had died because of it. Recalling how his father had protested when Samuel had insisted on joining the army, it now made perfect sense.

He couldn't bear it.

Angrily, he rose and swept everything from the top of the desk, sending all the various and sundry items crashing to the floor. Ink spilled over the carpet, the black stain spreading. It was a perfect metaphor for his father's life: a black stain that had spread out to encompass everything and everyone in his path. The destruction was oddly cathartic.

Moments later, the butler came knocking. "My lord, is aught amiss?"

Taking a deep and calming breath, Sinclair answered firmly, "It's fine. Everything is fine."

The butler opened the door, taking in the mess. "It is not fine, my lord. I've a note for you from Miss Hill. It was delivered by a messenger just moments ago. There is some urgency, I think."

Sinclair held out his hand for the note and then waved the butler away. He didn't read the note right away. He knew what it would say. He knew that within would be an apology, an assurance that she would always love him, and excuses that she had to marry as her family directed her to. But in the end, it would simply be a reiteration of the rejection she'd already presented him. The woman he loved was to marry another. And, in truth, he was content enough to let her do so. How could he marry her with the truth of his family's perfidy now hanging over his head?

Opening the note, he read the words penned so neatly.

MY DARLING,

I beg you to forgive me. If it were but my choice to marry for love rather than wed in the direction of my family's choosing, it would always be you. But, alas, I cannot. I am not free to love you as you deserve, but I am too selfish to let you go entirely. I pray you not forsake me, to hold me forever in your heart as I shall hold you in mine.

Whomever I may marry, know that in my heart you will always reside. I shall never not need you. I shall never not love you. And if freedom should find me, my first thought will be how quickly I may come to you.

Your love,

Charlotte

THEY WERE hollow and empty words. Because while he might love her, he knew her to be a liar.

"The carpet, my lord. If we do not clean it now, it will be ruined," the butler insisted.

Sinclair spared a glance for the still-spreading stain. "Let it. Let the whole damnable place fall to ruin."

CHAPTER ONE

1826

SINCLAIR STUMBLED over nothing in the inn yard. Losing his balance, he spun about, arms pinwheeling until he managed to right himself. *The world is spinning,* he thought, *and I am not.* Even when he'd come to a stop, the world had a topsy turvy feeling to it all.

He chuckled for a second, but that led to a wave of nausea which quickly banished his mirth. Swallowing thickly, he managed to stave off disaster. There was a willing woman awaiting him in a room upstairs. Casting up his accounts would certainly put a damper on his amorous plans for the evening.

Fumbling with the buttons at the fall of his breeches, he managed to release the fabric, and then relieved himself into the bushes at the edge of the yard. It was a far better option than any of the reeking chamber pots in the outdoor privies or the discreetly placed chamber pots inside. At least he was in the cool, fresh air.

He grinned as he thought of Nancy, the very eager and very buxom serving-girl for the establishment he'd elected to visit for the night. It was the only tavern in Boston Spa that had any sort of socialization. And company, though not necessarily carnal in nature, had been his sole pursuit that night. In truth, he'd simply wanted to not be alone with his own thoughts.

As for Nancy, she was a pretty enough thing. Cheeky and flirtatious, with an unparalleled bosom, she was never at a loss for attention. He'd never availed himself of her charms, but he'd come to the village that night seeking companionship, seeking a reprieve. She offered that in abundance.

Stumbling again, he righted himself. Looking up, he frowned. Clouds had drifted over the moon, leaving the inn yard completely dark. It was next to impossible to make out the shape of the buildings in the blackness. Staggering a bit, he moved toward one hulking shape, and when his hands connected with stone and wood, he grinned. Even drunk, he could find his way to a warm and willing woman.

Sidestepping, clinging to the ivy-covered bricks in an effort to keep himself reasonably vertical, he finally found the back door of the tavern. Reaching for the door handle, he had to fumble with the thing a bit until it finally opened. Stepping inside, he frowned. It was darker than he'd imagined, but then he realized he must have entered through a service door rather than the main door. The stairs leading up were narrow and dark, but Nancy had told him she'd be in the first room at the top of the stairs. She'd suggested she might even be waiting for him entirely naked.

Easing that door open, he stepped into a pitch-dark room. Squinting a bit, he could make out a large bed in the center of the chamber. The room was rather shockingly large. For a serving girl, it was positively palatial. *But perhaps the innkeeper was aware of just how many of his patrons would be spending time in Nancy's room*, he thought with a grin.

Making his way toward the bed, trying to be as quiet as possible, he removed his clothes along the way, dropping his cravat, his coat, and his waistcoat. Hobbling on one foot, he barely managed to stay upright as he tugged off one boot and then the other. At last, he dropped his trousers and stepped out of them. Reaching the bed, he lifted the sheets to climb into the narrow bed where the warm and curvaceous female body awaited him.

The mattress dipped beneath his weight, and that warm female body rolled toward him with a mildly alarmed squeak. As he caught her, wrapping his arms about her waist and tugging her bottom firmly against him, that squeak turned into a terrified shriek that threatened to split his skull completely open.

The most puzzling thing wasn't that she was screaming in his ear. It was that she was wrapped head to toe in heavy cotton. Why in heavens name would a woman who entertained gentlemen for a bit of coin, be wearing such a garment?

ALTHEA PARKER HAD BEEN SLEEPING SOUNDLY in her bed. She'd been dreaming of silk gowns and chocolates, things her miserly father would never permit her to have even if they were within their meager budget. After long days of scrubbing the floors in the vicarage, imagining a life of luxury was something she would often do to help take her mind off her aching back and knees. Floor scrubbing was her father's idea of punishment. Any time she wasn't suitably pious or obedient, he'd suggest they looked dusty and that it wouldn't do for the vicarage to be deemed slovenly.

It had been during that dream of decadent chocolates that she'd been rudely jolted awake by the weight of another person settling into her bed. Confused at first, she'd thought perhaps she was still dreaming. It was only as she'd tumbled toward them and reality intruded fully that she'd managed to make a sound. But when she'd felt strong arms close around her, pulling her against an obviously masculine frame in an unmistakably intimate manner, fear had settled in quickly. Realizing what was happening, Thea had screamed down the heavens.

The room was so dark she had no notion of who had forced their way into her bedroom. In truth, she had only the vaguest of ideas what this person's intentions might be. In short, she knew only enough to be terrified. But as she struggled to get away from him, he simply held her more firmly, his hands moving over her night rail as he muttered in what appeared to be confusion.

Please, do not let Father have consumed too much brandy. Please, do not let this stranger do unspeakable things to me while I scream for help that will not come.

It wasn't a formal prayer by any stretch. But the lord knew her heart, and those urgent requests were made with genuine feeling and a great deal of faith and humility.

Perhaps for the first time in her life, the Lord did actually answer her prayers. Within seconds of her ear-splitting screams, her father kicked in the door to her chamber. He stood there in his patched dressing gown and cap, with a lamp clutched in one hand and a fireplace poker in the other.

"What is this? What sort of wickedness is taking place under my roof? Explain yourself, Althea!"

It took her a moment to realize that, although a strange man had burst in to their home and climbed into her bed, quite literally scaring her half to death, her father was assuming she was a willing party to the lot of it. If she hadn't still been clasped in the embrace of a very naked man who had been invited into neither her chamber nor her bed, she might have been insulted by that. As it was, she was a bit too preoccupied to really take that in.

"I didn't invite him here, Father! Would I have screamed for help if I'd wanted him in here?" she demanded.

As if recognizing the sense in that, her father then turned his attention to the man in her bed. "Sir, you will unhand my daughter and remove yourself from her bed immediately!"

"I will happily unhand her, but as my trousers are on the floor, I think my getting out of this bed would not be recommended," the words were slurred but the speech was unmistakably aristocratic and terribly familiar.

With her back pressed to his chest, she hadn't seen his face. But she knew that voice. It couldn't possibly be.

He leaned his head closer to her to whisper in her ear. "I take it I wandered into the side door of the vicarage rather than the side door of the tavern...and that your name, my dear, is not Nancy?"

She was not Nancy. But she knew precisely who and what Nancy was, and her face flamed in humiliation. But before she could reply, another commotion occurred. It was at that moment that her private shame became public.

Apparently, her scream had been loud enough to attract the notice of the tavern's patrons. Several of them came rushing up the stairs, brandishing weapons, to find her naked in bed with none other than Sinclair Wortham, Lord Mayville.

CHAPTER TWO

The morning after

BLEARY EYED, with a splitting headache, a turning stomach, and his heart pounding like a team of black-smiths at the forge, Sinclair stood before the vicar and recited his vows. Beside him, his mouse of a bride recited hers as well. Her voice was soft and low pitched, and she only shed a few tears. His recklessness, *his drunkenness*, had done that. Whatever her hopes and dreams for a future had been, whatever thoughts of marrying some simple vicar or cleric she might have had, had been irrevocably destroyed by him.

"And now you are husband and wife," the vicar said, snapping his prayer book closed in a decisive and most displeased manner. "May God have mercy on you both."

It was not uttered as a benediction. That much was clearly obvious. The vicar was quite put out with him but seemed far more put out with his unfortunate daughter. Perhaps being forced to marry him wasn't the worst thing in the world. She might have had to continue on under the less-than-caring eye of her father. The vicar was beyond cold, and he couldn't imagine that it was just their current and somewhat scandalous circumstances that resulted in his icy demeanor.

As they signed the register, silence reigned supreme. Not even a breath was heard in the sanctuary. The witnesses, the local physician and the innkeeper, stepped forward to do the same.

"And you need not think to come crawling back to the vicarage," the vicar continued with his malicious disdain. "I've washed my hands of you, girl. I'll not have you shaming me further."

Beside him, his bride was stonily silent. She didn't acknowledge her father's disownment of her. But, then, she didn't acknowledge him either. Somehow, she seemed to be quite above the entire fiasco. A simple vicar's daughter or not, she'd mastered the art of quiet dignity.

He offered his arm to escort her from the church. She glanced down at it then up at him to meet his gaze. After a not-so-subtle hesitation, she placed her hand on his arm and allowed him to lead her from the church, to his waiting carriage. As they left the building, he spared a glance at her profile.

She was not a beauty. There was nothing particularly striking in her features, though they were pleasant enough. She had dark brows that did nicely set off her eyes, which he thought were blue, though he couldn't be entirely sure. In all, she was pretty, but not extraordinary.

It could be worse. At least he wasn't saddled with a crow.

Helping her into the carriage, he climbed in after and let out a weary groan. His entire body hurt after his ridiculous night of excess. It was a night that would live in infamy in their small village, and the consequences of it were life altering—quite literally, until death would they part.

"The house will be a bit of a surprise to you," he warned. "It's in shambles."

"I can set it to rights," she said with soft assurance.

He smiled. "I'm sure you can. But I do not wish for it to be set to rights. I wish nothing more than for the entire structure to fall into ruin and be reclaimed by the earth. It is naught but a mausoleum to misery, regardless."

"You do not wish for me to set your house to rights?" she asked.

"No. I'm certain there are other things you can occupy yourself with," he replied.

"On the contrary, my lord. As a woman, my entire life has been devoted to learning the skills that would allow me to maintain my husband's home. If I am not to do so, I've frankly no notion what else I would do."

"We shall endeavor to find you something, then. Perhaps the first thing we should do is see to your wardrobe. I've not been to London in ages, and I do have numerous family members to irritate with news of my nuptials," he said. "If you're game, that is."

"I've never been to London," she said softly. "I've always longed to see it."

Satisfied that his new wife would not find their union entirely miserable and regrettable, Sinclair laid his head against the seat back and promptly fell asleep.

———————

THERE WERE SO many thoughts whirling in Thea's mind that she couldn't even make sense of them all. She'd gone to bed a dowdy spinster just the night before, and now she was a baroness, Lady Mayville. Still dowdy, for the moment at least, but no longer a spinster.

Surreptitiously, she surveyed her sleeping husband's face. While still handsome beyond measure, there was no doubt his excesses of the previous night had taken a toll. His pallor was not the normal sun-kissed shade she'd grown accustomed to seeing when she chanced to pass him in the village. Whiskers shadowed the firm line of his jaw, and there were dark circles spreading beneath the thick fan of his lashes where they rested. None of that managed to alter the fact that she found him astoundingly beautiful.

For all the time she had been living in poverty and obscurity in Boston Spa, she'd been well aware of him. Every chance encounter, every glimpse of him in a shop, on the street, or at the rare social gathering he attended, she'd been struck by how perfect he was. And in all that time, when she'd been pining for him, building fantasies about him miraculously falling in love with her like something from a fairy story, he hadn't even known her name. When he'd recited it in the church, he'd fumbled it abominably. It stung her pride, but it didn't surprise her.

Turning her gaze away from him, Thea focused on the countryside instead. It was a safer subject for contemplation. This would not be a happy union, of that she was certain. No couple could enter into wedlock where one was loved and the other invisible and not have it end in misery.

It didn't take long to reach his estate.

Rosedale Manor.

Recalling what he'd said about it, about his desire to let it fall into decay, Thea frowned. It had always seemed such a lovely house to her, despite the air of neglect that hovered about it. She'd thought perhaps it only needed a woman's touch, a mistress to make it into a proper home. But that was not to be. Was he impoverished? Was there some secret debt or reversal of fortune that had occurred? She didn't think so. His clothes were perfectly tailored and in the latest fashion. Nothing in his personal effects gave the indication of being worn and tattered. His horses and equipage were all in top form. So why?

"You're thinking very loudly."

He'd spoken without ever opening his eyes. His head was still tipped back against the seat, his hands clasped in front of him.

"Rosedale Manor is lovely."

"It is. But so are many rotten apples," Mayville remarked.

"Who is it that you are punishing by letting it fall to ruin?" she asked pointedly.

At that, he did open his eyes. He leveled an inscrutable glance at her, its meaning completely hidden from her. "Myself, I suppose. You will find I am a perverse creature, Lady Mayville."

He hadn't used her newly acquired title out of a desire for formality or even as a means of acknowledging their union. He'd done so, she thought, because he couldn't recall her name. With another sigh, Thea turned away from him again and pinned her attention firmly on the horizon.

CHAPTER THREE

They entered Rosedale Manor and were greeted by his butler. Had he known he'd be returning with a wife in tow, he could have had the servants lined up to greet her properly. But it was an unforeseen circumstance beyond all prediction.

It would have been a very small line of servants, at any rate. It was quite remarkable how one could economize on household servants when one wished to let the house rot around them. They saw to his comfort, providing meals and cleaning the chambers that he used on a daily basis. He'd made it a point that no wallpaper, no carpets, no draperies or furniture should be replaced, no matter how worn and tattered they were. If windows broke, boards were placed over them. If shutters came loose, they were simply left to bang at the stone walls. I roof tiles blew off, so long as the intruding water did not impede his comfort, they were left as is. And still the house soldiered on, seemingly impervious to the elements and his intentional neglect. It mocked him.

"Havens, this is your new mistress, Alice, Lady Mayville," Sinclair stated. He could see the butler's expression shifting with surprise, but only slightly. The man would never be so common as to appear as flabbergasted as he surely must be.

"Althea," she corrected softly. "Althea, Lady Mayville."

He closed his eyes even as he felt a flush of embarrassment creeping up his neck. How the hell had he married her and still didn't know her bloody name? "Of course, forgive me. Althea. It's been a long night and a longer morning yet." To the butler, he instructed, "Please have cook prepare a small repast and have it laid in the breakfast room for my wife. Then instruct Mrs. Whitman to give Lady Mayville a tour of the house so that she may instruct her on which areas of it are safe or to be avoided. I mean to seek my bed and try to recover from the last eighteen hours."

It was probably a mistake. No, it was definitely a mistake. The moment he said it, he knew he'd made another terrible error. But he was just so damned tired he couldn't even think. It was his own fault—all of it. Hopefully, after a few hours of uninterrupted sleep, he'd be able to say something to her that wasn't entirely offensive...and be able to remember her name. Blast it all.

"Forgive me, Lady Mayville. I shall see you at dinner." And with that, he headed for the stairs, leaving her in the capable hands of his likely shocked servants.

AND JUST LIKE THAT, Althea was alone. With only a single valise containing her few meager gowns and the personal possessions her father had permitted her to take with her, she stood in the once-grand entry of Rosedale Hall, like a beggar asking for scraps.

"Your ladyship," the butler said, bowing. "Allow me to show you to your chamber. You may refresh yourself, and then a light repast will be available for you. I'm afraid the chamber...well, we were not expecting you. It will not be your permanent chamber, but a guest room that has recently been aired."

"I'm certain it's fine. Thank you," Thea replied. Could it all be any more humiliating? Her husband—well, not even that, really, so much as the stranger she had married—didn't even know her name, for heaven's sake!

The butler took her small valise and led the way up the staircase. Footmen were in short supply in the house, it seemed. The treads creaked ominously, but the wood felt firm enough beneath her feet. Of course, when she reached the landing, there was white dust on the floor where a bit of plaster had fallen.

"It's the damp. We lose a bit more of that frieze with each rain." The butler pointed to an elaborate scene on the ceiling above. "My apologies, your ladyship."

"Do not apologize, Havens. You are doing as your employer has bid you. Following orders, even when they seem to lack any sort of sense, does not require any sort of apology."

The butler nodded. "He is not what you think he is, my lady. There are reasons for what he has done here, even if we are not privy to them. Please do not think poorly of him."

Thea heard the imploring note in the man's voice and sighed. "I will not think badly of him for his choices about this house, Havens. That is all I can promise."

The butler nodded, and they continued along the corridor. He showed her into a room that was neat and tidy. It did not have the same air of neglect and decay that she sensed in other areas of the house. It smelled fresh, and there was no dust to be seen. "This will do nicely, Havens. Thank you. Please inform the cook and house-keeper that I will be down in half an hour."

"Yes, my lady," he said, and exited the room.

Alone, Thea picked up her bag and took out the few dresses she owned and shook the worst of the wrinkles out of them. Placing them in the intricately carved wardrobe, she noted how shabby they looked against the fine furniture. They would fit right in with the remainder of the house, at least.

With that done, she began unpacking her toiletries. Again, there weren't many. Her father had frowned upon any sort of vanity. She had a small bottle of scent that had been a gift from her aunt. There was a small box of hair pins. Her father permitted the heavy tortoise-shell pins and combs because, with the heaviness of her very thick hair, they were a necessity to appear tidy, rather than just for the sake of appearance. Her only possession of any real value was the cameo parure that had been her mother's. She'd been permitted to keep it but had never once worn the jewelry within that leather case.

It took a very small amount of time to unpack her belongings. Seating herself at the writing desk before the window, she opened the drawer and found the materials needed. Penning a short letter to her aunt, she explained that she had married. Electing not to go into too much detail about the events necessitating the union, she simply described it as "quite sudden."

With that task completed, she sprinkled sand over the page and carefully folded it, sealing it with the wax found in the drawer. Tucking it into her pocket, she considered how lowering it was that she'd have to ask her husband for money to even see the letter mailed. The small amount of savings she'd managed to amass had been taken by her father. He'd deemed them unnecessary, given that she had managed to ensnare a wealthy husband.

Thea couldn't stop her eyes from rolling. Her father often saw what was convenient for him. He wanted her savings, so she'd ensured a wealthy husband. He hadn't wanted to pay for a housekeeper and cook, so her "complete unattractiveness," as he'd put it, had been a generous gift from the lord. There was always a way for him to twist the situation to support having just what he wanted from it. He might have been a vicar, but he was as far from holy as any man could be. Of course, the same was said of her new husband. Many people spoke of his wickedness, of his perfidy, that he was a rake far beyond redemption. But she'd watched him in the village. He was kind to those when he had no reason to be. His drunkenness was cause for concern, but at least he wasn't a violent drunk, looking to brawl with anyone who would raise fists with him.

Leaving her temporary chamber, she could see a flurry of activity at the end of the corridor. There were two maids rushing in and out of a chamber, each carrying an armload of linens. It was the master suite, then. His room would be on the other side. She hadn't allowed herself to consider what would happen when he was sober enough to think of consummating their union.

How many times had she imagined that he would look at her? How many times had she seen him in their small village and wished that, just for a single second, his gaze would turn toward her, and he would see her? And now all she wanted was to disappear.

CHAPTER FOUR

Sinclair stared at his reflection in the washstand mirror as he tied his cravat. He didn't need the mirror to tell him he looked like shite. He felt it all the way to his bones. Drunkenness had not robbed him of his memory in this case. Every second of the night before now played over in his mind. It had been the stumbling in the darkness— drunk, disoriented, so cocked up he didn't know his right from his left. He'd gotten himself turned around and wandered into the vicarage, traumatizing the innocent daughter of the local parson rather than climbing into the bed of a woman who was well acquainted with the appetites of men.

"Christ almighty," he muttered. And he still couldn't remember her name. *Alice. Anna. Alma?* "Why the devil do so many female names start with the letter A?"

With his cravat done, he straightened his waistcoat and headed for the door. He paused there to take a steadying breath and then made his way below stairs to the drawing room, where he would greet his new wife and try to figure out how they were going to manage. Annulment was not outside the realm of possibility. He could certainly afford to set her up in a house somewhere and provide her a decent living.

With that thought uppermost in his mind, he descended the stairs and entered one of the few reasonably comfortable rooms in the entire house. She was already there, seated in one of the straight-backed chairs that flanked the fireplace. Dressed plainly in a simple gown of some muddy, indeterminate color, he took his first honest look at her when he wasn't either dead drunk or miserably hungover.

She was not a beauty. Passably pretty would be a description applied to her by some. But she was the sort of woman who, in a crowded ballroom amongst other ladies, would disappear. That had little to do with her features and far more to do with her demeanor. Quiet, reserved, and self-contained, she was the sort who would have enjoyed her wallflower status, free from all the expectations of inane chatter.

Under his regard, she never squirmed. But when she'd had enough of it, she did lift her chin as she said, "I am not a specimen to be studied, sir."

"Sinclair. My name is Sinclair. As we are now married, I cannot imagine a reasonable excuse for not utilizing it. Sherry?" he asked, crossing the room to where a tray of libations had been placed.

"I do not care for it, thank you."

Prim, proper, poised. *Judgmental.* "Ah, there's the good vicar's influence. I can hear it in your disapproval."

"What you hear is my distaste for sherry. If you choose to interpret it as more than that, I cannot be responsible for it."

"What is your name again?" he asked, as he poured himself a drink.

"Althea." There was certainly a note of exasperation in her voice then.

"Althea," he repeated, testing it on his tongue. Looking back at her, he shook his head. "No. That won't do. You most certainly are not an Althea. Don't you have some sort of nickname or diminutive that your friends and family use?"

"I have no friends. And my father, the vicar you hold in such dislike, is my only family," she admitted.

He considered it carefully. "Thea, then. I shall call you Thea. Surely I can remember it if it is of my choosing."

"One would think," she intoned sourly. "I am not a dog, sir, to be renamed at the whim of whomever happens to be responsible for feeding me."

Ignoring her displeasure at his choice of shortening her name, he moved back to the settee near where she had perched on her chair with precise and rigid posture. "Tell me, Thea, what shall we do about this mess?"

"This mess? Do you mean our marriage?" she asked. At his nod, she shook her head in dismay. "How in heaven's name should I know what to do? You, with your drunkenness and poor sense of direction, have wrought this entire debacle."

"Well, it isn't entirely my fault," he insisted. "You are the one who screamed, after all."

She parted her lips, her eyes narrowed and her chest heaving with temper. Her cheeks flushed with it as well. And in that moment, she was, he thought, more than just passably pretty. In a fit of temper, she was actually quite lovely. Or perhaps he was simply a perverse creature incapable of appreciating a woman who didn't loathe him.

After a second's hesitation, she reined in her temper and calmly stated, "I will not be goaded into a divorce or annulment. I doubt there is anything you might do that would make my life so unbearable as the incessant abuse and poverty of the vicarage. Even if this house is a mausoleum to decay."

He couldn't stop the grin that spread across his face at her acerbic reply. "You are remarkably astute, Lady Mayville...Thea."

"I warn you, my lord, I will not be humiliated by being cast out to live separately either. Perhaps after a time, arrangements can be made. But I have been humiliated by your carelessness enough as it stands," she stated. "I am not what you wished for in a wife, and you, sir, are most assuredly not what I wished for in a husband. But we must, for the time being, make the best of it."

"And what consequences will there be if I do not come to heel?"

She smiled tightly. "I shall hire servants to clean your

house. I shall hire workman to paint and paper your walls. I shall devote my every moment to undoing your willful neglect of this home."

It was just devious enough to earn his grudging respect.

"Let us have dinner, Thea," he murmured, "and ponder our now-linked fates."

CHAPTER FOUR

Whether it had been her threat to set his house to rights or something else that she could not fathom, their shared dinner went far better than their interaction in the drawing room. He stopped being intentionally goading and settled into something that might have been deemed pleasant had she not been waiting for the other shoe to drop. That was in part due to his earlier behavior and in part because it was simply how she had grown used to living.

Her father, a man of the cloth, was the least holy of men she had ever encountered. Miserly, mean spirited, belittling, and quite often simply brutish, he'd trained her to expect the worst. A smile could precede the most vicious, cutting remarks or even a slap.

How many times had she dreamed of living elsewhere? Had anything but poverty and degradation awaited her, she'd have fled his home long ago. But at least as the vicar's spinster daughter she had respectability. Women without family connections and little to no money did not do well in the world.

Althea glanced at the man who was now her husband —the man who held all the power in their current situation. He was entitled to beat and abuse her as he chose. Yet, barring a strange and strained conversation about their future and his willingness to bestow a new name upon her rather than bothering to recall the one she possessed, he seemed to have little interest in her.

Dessert, a simple tart with berries and cream, had just been served, when there was a loud commotion. A couple burst in, the man handsome with dark hair and the woman impossibly beautiful with a wealth of jet-black hair that seemed to defy nature. They were both very fashionably dressed, with the kind of town polish that she saw only rarely. Of course, they were known to her. As the vicar's daughter, everyone was known to her. It was Mr. Dudley Blakemore and his wife, Lady Helena Blakemore, sister to the Earl of Winburn.

"Mayville, we heard the most ridiculous rumor in town while dining with the Cardwells!" Mr. Blakemore was calling out. "They said—"

He never finished the statement, as Lady Helena Blakemore had promptly shoved her elbow directly into her husband's gut, leaving him bent forward and gasping. "Some rumors do, in fact, have a foundation in truth, it would seem," Lady Helena said serenely. "I take it you are Althea, Lady Mayville?"

"I am," Althea said.

Lady Helena sailed forward, so graceful and elegant

it seemed her feet dared not touch the carpet less they be soiled by it in some way. "Then, I bid you welcome to our small family. I realize not everyone is aware that my dear husband is Mayville's nephew."

"I wasn't aware Lord Mayville had any siblings, at all," Althea remarked. "No doubt, as gossip has informed you, our nuptials were somewhat expedited."

"Expedited," Lady Helena mused. "That is certainly a very polite description. I will make no bones about it, Lady Mayville, I fear you have been done very shabbily by your husband and by the people of this village who permitted such a thing to occur. For shame, my lord. No woman should have to marry in such a havycavy manner."

"You did," Mayville replied. "The pair of you hied off to Gretna Green, and I do believe you were wearing breeches."

Lady Helena smiled. "Yes, but I am a hoyden. And your bride is a genteel woman of breeding and taste. There is a distinct difference. I adore being shocking and breaking rules simply for the sake of having done so. I daresay we are cut from very different cloths. But, alas, we were speaking of family connections. My husband's mother was Lord Mayville's older half-sister from their mother's first marriage. They were not close, were you, Mayville?"

"No, we were not. But my nephew is rather stubborn —like a pox, really."

Mr. Blakemore simply laughed. "You are terrible when your misdeeds catch up to you, uncle. But let us go to your study and have brandy and cigars while my wife entreats yours to become a reformer."

Mayville rose reluctantly and followed the other man from the room. He paused at the door, looking back at her for a moment in question, almost as if he was reluctant to leave her to the potentially less-than-tender mercies of Lady Helena. But then he shook his head and strode purposefully through the door.

Immediately, Lady Helena settled into his vacated seat and availed herself of his freshly served dessert. "This looks delicious. The Cardwells never have good sweets. I don't know why we continue to dine with them. Lady Cardwell is so obsessed with eating 'healthful' foods that it's really quite dreadful. No rich sauces. Lots of liver and spices that one of her highland nurses insisted were wondrous for one's fertility."

Althea blinked. "You discuss such things with her?"

Lady Helena smiled. "Being a married woman dramatically alters the scope of one's conversational topics, you will find. And I wouldn't have discussed such a thing with her except that she was very kind to me when Dudley and I first married. And I have recently discovered that I am enceinte," she confided, the last word a mere whisper.

"Oh. I see," Althea said. But a pang of longing ignited within her. A dream she'd held for so many years and had finally let go of suddenly revived before her. All she had wanted when she was younger was a family of her own.

"Well, regardless, there are certain foods and certain spices that Lady Cardwell is eating to improve her fertility but that I must not, in my current state, consume. So, half of the menu had to be avoided tonight, and I'm positively famished. Is there more of this tart?"

Althea had no idea. But, luckily, Lady Helena felt at home enough to simply wave to a footman and request more of the decadent dessert if it was available.

"Did he really sneak into your bedchamber?" Lady Helena asked.

Struggling to follow the ever-changing topics of conversation, Althea nodded. "Yes, he did. He was quite intoxicated, I believe."

"Well, that's not unusual these days. But you could be good for him, I think. He needs to not rattle around all alone in this hovel he's creating."

"I'm rather more concerned at the moment, Lady Helena, with whether or not he will be good for me," Althea replied.

At that Lady Helena blanched. Immediately, she sat down her fork. "Oh my goodness. I'm just prattling on here as if you ought to be happy about all this. I am sorry. Did you have hopes in another direction, then?"

What a terribly worded question that was. It cast a very stark light on both her life before and her current situation. "No, Lady Helena. I had no hopes. Not then and not now."

***

"THE VICAR'S DAUGHTER, UNCLE? REALLY?"

Mayville sipped his brandy and glared at his nephew,

a man his junior only by a matter of days. "Would you stop calling me Uncle as if I were in my dotage? Don't be an arse, Dudley. It doesn't suit you."

"You only call me Dudley when you're annoyed," Blakemore insisted.

"Then, you should take it as a warning."

"What will you do? Pack her off to London with a generous allowance and instructions not to embarrass the family? Except, of course, this family and embarrassment tend to go hand in hand."

"She will not go. Not immediately, at any rate. She's stated that I've humiliated her enough without packing her off to live elsewhere."

Blakemore nodded sagely. "She isn't wrong. The gossip in town is not good. It paints her in a far-less-than-innocent light, you know?"

He didn't know. How would he know? He'd spent the better part of the day sleeping off a hangover. "How on earth could anyone presume it would be her fault? I invaded her bedchamber and mistook her for a willing and easily bought tavern wench! Damn and blast."

The room grew silent. Blakemore looked away, clearly uncomfortable.

"What is it you aren't telling me?" Mayville demanded.

"It's her father. Most of the gossip has been stirred by him. He's telling anyone who will listen that she's wicked, sly, lazy... That she planned all of this from the start. The man is an utter prig. Anyone who's ever had to sit through one of his sermons knows him to be a hypocrite and a bore. But he still holds sway in the village. People will not be kind to her when she returns to the village because he does not wish them to be, and all they want is to curry favor."

Mayville leaned back in his chair. His headache from earlier in the day was returning. And it had nothing, for once, to do with drink. "You think I should take her to London."

"I think you should take her *somewhere*, at least till things have died down. But you can't molder away in here forever. You certainly shouldn't expect her to. Perhaps she'll like London so well she will decide to stay there, even when you are ready to return home."

"That, Blakemore, is one of the more sensible things I have ever heard you say. I shall take her to London. I shall outfit her as the most fashionable of ladies and launch her into society. She will have all the friends and social engagements she might ever want. And then I can return here to rusticate in my willful decay, as she put it."

Blakemore grinned. "Just don't tell Helena what you're about. If she thinks you mean to abandon the girl, it won't go well for you."

"Come to think of it, why are you advocating my abandonment of her? It's shockingly unlike you, with all those very inconvenient morals you possess."

Blakemore shrugged. "As someone who cares for you, it's very difficult to watch you destroy this house and yourself in equal measure and enthusiasm. I should very much hate for that innocent young woman to be charmed into feeling something for you so that she might then watch you drink and debauch your way into an early grave. I do believe, Uncle, that she deserves better than you. Given that she's had to endure the vicar for all these years, there ought to be some reward for her."

It stung. It was the truth, certainly. But still it stung. She did deserve better.

CHAPTER FIVE

After years of dreaming of it, she was finally on her way to London. Of course, in her dreams, she'd been going off to London to have a season, to wear beautiful dresses and dance in the arms of gallant and handsome men. One of those men would have fallen madly in love with her and become her husband. Well, she had a husband. He was handsome. He was hardly gallant, however, and he most assuredly was not in love with her.

Mayville, as everyone called him, was slumbering peacefully on the carriage seat opposite her. It gave her an opportunity to study him far more closely than she ever had in the past. He'd always been impossibly handsome. She could recall a dozen fantasies of what he might be like, but they bore little similarity to the man who was actually her husband. Snide, sometimes rude, often flippant and dismissive, he seemed to think his behavior impacted no one—and no one, conversely, was permitted to impact his behavior.

They had been married for four days. For four nights, she had slept alone. He'd never come to her bed. He'd never kissed her or even touched her beyond escorting her to dinner, and even then he sometimes simply walked at her side. It should not have stung her pride. She was used to being considered plain, after all. Her entire life she'd had that drilled into her head repeatedly. She was too plain to attract a husband and too poor to get one either. There was no need to spend money on dresses that would flatter her, as it would be trying to make a silk purse from a sow's ear.

As always, thoughts of her father's cruelty and disapproval darkened her already bitter mood. With a sigh, she turned her attention back to her husband's face. Yes, he was handsome. But the lifestyle he'd chosen for himself was beginning to take a toll. There were fine lines at the corners of his eyes and deeper grooves still at the corners of his mouth. Dark circles ringed his eyes, and she knew that he slept very little.

"What was it you said?" he asked softly. "Ah, yes. 'I am not a specimen to be examined.'"

"Touché."

His eyes opened then, slightly bleary but still a startling shade of icy blue that she'd never seen on anyone else. "Do I have something on my face? Did I miss a spot of shaving soap, perhaps?"

"You haven't shaved," she replied.

"Then, it would be doubly miraculous for it to have survived intact for so many hours. How very tenacious of it. To what, Lady Mayville, do I owe your remarkable curiosity about my face?" he asked drolly.

"It isn't about your face. It's about you as a whole, I suppose. You are something of a mystery, my lord," she mused. "Why is it that you love all the vices that can be found so freely in London, and yet you choose to avoid London altogether? Until now, of course, which only begs another question: Why now? Why go to London now? Do you mean to break your word and seek an annulment? Or simply abandon me there to fend for myself?"

"I've never given my word that I would not seek an annulment," he answered. "As for my distaste for London, I think it has far more to do with the company I would be forced to keep there. As to why now, I shall not lie to you about it. Your father was not content to see you ruined at my hands; now he would have your reputation shredded beyond repair at his own hands. He's telling all who will listen in Boston Spa that you are an adventuress who set out to ensnare me. And, so, removing us to London for the time being seemed prudent."

Althea blinked at that. She hadn't conversed with anyone in town. The only people she had spoken with were Mayville, his servants, and the Blakemores. It didn't surprise her, of course. Her father was a man who lived for misery. He loved to see it in others and revel in his own superiority.

"Well, that does make sense. Save for your decision to act with prudence. I daresay that was quite unusual."

He smirked at that, a quirking of his lips as one brow

lifted ever so slightly. "I think that you really ought to like me more, or at least pretend to, if you wish for us to remain married."

"Then, I suppose you ought to give me something to like. I have heard others say you are charming, but I have yet to see evidence of it," she remarked.

"Charming was a very long time ago. Now I am dissolute, debauched, drunken, and very often disorderly, hence our hasty marriage." He sat up then, folding his body forward in a graceful gesture until his elbows rested on his knees and the distance between them was significantly less. "But we shall not have an annulment. I have dealt very poorly with you. You are entirely innocent in all of this, and between my carelessness and your own father's viciousness, you are essentially ruined. To seek an annulment would leave you a pariah among any sort of genteel or noble society. So, we shall remain husband and wife...though I cannot say we shall always reside under one roof. In truth, I cannot attest to how much longer the roof will last at Rosedale. Perhaps it will collapse upon its careless overseer and leave you a young and wealthy widow."

She shook her head vigorously. "Do not speak so casually of your death. That is not something that should be considered even in jest, my lord."

"I was not jesting. But I will not speak of it again, as it clearly troubles you so. Tell me, Thea, what would you enjoy in London? Balls? The theatre? Art and museums? Perhaps garden parties or intellectual salons?"

"I don't really want any of those things," she said. "I

thought I did when I was younger, but now, at my age, I wouldn't even know how to begin adjusting to such social demands."

He frowned at that, considering her response. "Then, what is it that you do want?"

The pang of longing she'd felt at Lady Helena's confession several nights earlier returned to her then as it had done so many times since then. "I want a child."

IF SHE HAD ASKED for the moon, he would not have been more surprised. Trying not to allow his shock to be too apparent, he asked with aplomb, "I presume you are not entirely ignorant of how such a thing would be achieved."

Her blush was answer enough, but despite her discomfort, she did not look away. "I am aware. I realize that all you want is to be rid of me. It is not uncommon in society marriages for a couple to live separate lives once they have children—"

"Not children, Thea. Sons. Heirs. Of which I never intended to have any."

"But your title..."

He shrugged. "The title can hang. While I do not have the same animosity towards it as I do the family seat, it's not very important to me either. But that is all you require for us to lead our separate lives?"

"Yes," she said softly. "I would happily live in London or Bath. Far from you. Far from my father. I presume that you would provide at least a respectable living for myself and the child we might have."

"*You* might have. The child would be entirely your responsibility. I'd be little more than a sire, after all. And the child would probably be better for it," he answered.

She clenched her hands in her lap. It was the only outward sign of just how affected she was by their very strange conversation. "You are in agreement?"

"Not exactly," he said. "I'm willing to consider it. We'll discuss it more once we've settled in London for a time."

She only nodded in response and then lapsed into complete silence as she stared out the window at the passing scenery.

Mayville studied her, feeling that it was his due. She was an enigma, his wife. Cold and reserved at times, angry and snappish at others, with no desire to move about in society, and her fondest wish was to be a mother. She was one contradiction after another. Though he had hardly given her reason to be anything less. He had not made an effort to know her, preferring to think of their situation as only temporary. Of course, it wasn't. Their living arrangements might be, but she'd be his wife until one of them shuffled off the mortal coil.

"Did he strike you?" he asked.

"My father?" she countered.

"Yes. I would hardly ask about anyone else. I never liked him, but I rarely like any member of the clergy," he commented.

"I daresay many of them hold you in a high degree of

contempt as well," she mused. "You'd confound them endlessly with your penchant for self destruction and your complete antipathy of salvation of any sort."

It was a truth he could not and would not deny. But it was also an effort on her part to avoid the question. "Answer the question, Thea."

"Yes. On occasion...when he felt it was warranted."

"And when was that? Daily?"

"Weekly, I suppose. Sometimes more and sometimes less. I should have been content to scrub the floors and prepare his meals while he rattled on endlessly about original sin and the inherent wickedness of all females. He never knew what to make of me and my love of books and literature. It was something he felt most women should avoid. Taxing our brains would lead us into fits of hysteria."

Rebellion, more like. Not that he had a problem with rebellious women. They were generally the most entertaining sort. "He was very cruel to you, wasn't he?"

"He said very cruel things. I would far rather tolerate a slap or a shove than the sharp sting of his cutting tongue," she admitted. "But if I'm to tell you all of my dark and bitter secrets, I will ask for yours in return. Are you prepared for that sort of reciprocity, my lord?"

"I'll tell you almost anything that you ask," he agreed. "But only if you stop 'my-lording' me all the time. My name is Mayville. Or even Sinclair if you so choose."

"Very well, Sinclair. Why do you wish to see your ancestral home crumble to ruin before your eyes?"

Mayville blinked at that. She had certainly gone for

the jugular. "The precision of a surgeon in conversation, wife. I discovered, upon my inheritance of it, that it was a house that had been bought and paid for with the blood of innocents. The men of my family had violated every code of honor imaginable to fund their lavish lifestyles. And I see nothing noble in preserving it. That is all I mean to say on the subject."

"Then, let us enjoy the silence. It is a pretty after-noon, and I have seen little of the countryside outside of Boston Spa. I should like to know what more than one tiny corner of England looks like."

CHAPTER SIX

It was the last night of their journey, but the weather had turned. The sunshine had given way to great torrents of rain, and they'd been forced to seek shelter at an inn north of London. The White Hart at Welwyn was small and very crowded. Standing near the door of the taproom, waiting for her husband to procure their lodgings for the night, the rowdy atmosphere made her feel unaccountably anxious. The boisterous voices and the clanging of tankards against scarred wooden tables left her rattled.

It hadn't escaped her notice that everyone had stared when they entered the room. Every place they had stopped along the journey, the reaction had been the same. He, with his obvious aristocratic lineage and well-tailored clothing, looked very much at odds next to her, in her shabby, drab garments and work-roughened hands. She could feel people staring at them both, from him to her and back again, as they tried to make sense of why the two might be together. Surely a less likely married couple had never been seen.

He doesn't want to be married to you, regardless. That traitorous thought intruded in her mind, reminding her of all the reasons their current predicament was a disaster. The school-girl crush she had harbored for him—back when she'd only seen him from a distance and thought him wealthy and handsome and slightly wicked—had faded. He was too complex for such simple feelings to ever be sustained in his presence. She wasn't even certain she liked him, let alone wished to be his wife. But wishes were irrelevant, as the deed was done, and all that was left was to make the best of it, whether they lived under one roof or if the breadth and length of England separated them.

At that moment, a loud bark of laughter was followed by an equally loud curse and a thud as one man knocked another to the floor. Beneath her simple woolen cloak, Althea crossed her arms, hugging them tightly about herself to still her shaking. It was the sort of place her father had often warned her against—the sort of place he'd told her she'd wind up serving far more than just ale if she dared leave his house.

A moment later, Sinclair returned to her. He carried a single key in his hand, and his expression was bleak.

"They've only one room left. They're holding court here tomorrow," he explained, "which means the crowd is here mostly for petty complaints and offenses. It isn't safe for you to be alone anyway."

"I do not care. I just want out of this taproom," she insisted.

He frowned at that but nodded in agreement, leading her up the stairs. "I realize that I am a failure at being a husband, Thea, but I'm not going to let anything happen to you either. You are safe enough."

She believed him, but it would be much easier to feel safe when there was a heavy door between her and the raucous clientele of the White Hart. Following closely behind him, she reached for his coat, clutching the fabric in her hand. At the top of the stairs, he turned to the right and led them down to the end of the corridor. The door was so low he had to duck to enter the room. Once inside, she realized it wasn't just the door. The room had a low, sloped ceiling.

"This is certainly cozy."

"For very short people and young children, I think it would be," he agreed. "For myself, I'll have developed a hunchback by morning."

She smiled tightly at his jest. "Then, you should most certainly take the bed. I can sleep on the floor and spare your aching back."

"Most certainly not. I might be dissolute, debauched, dissipated—some might even go so far as to call me an inveterate rogue—but I have never in my life made a woman, certainly not a gently bred woman, sleep on the floor."

It would not have been the first time. Forcing her to sleep near the kitchen hearth had been one of her father's favorite punishments for her. Whenever she had failed to clean the kitchen to his specifications or prepared a meal that he found lacking, he would lock her bedroom door and deny her access to its comforts. Somehow, she thought relaying that particular detail to her husband would not be well received.

"We will share the bed," he said.

Althea wanted to protest. But, in truth, there was no good reason to do so. He was her husband. There was nothing inherently improper about them sharing a bed, despite the rather unusual nature of their married state.

"Will you step outside so that I might prepare for bed?" She asked.

"No. But I will turn around. I'm too bloody tired to care about your modesty or your state of undress," he admitted, turning his back to her and settling on the edge of the bed to remove his boots.

Althea huffed out a breath in annoyance. "You most certainly are not a gentleman."

"Indeed, I am not. If I were, circumstances would never have led us here," he remarked carelessly.

Shrugging out of her cloak, she draped it over the chair to dry. Her hands trembled with both nerves and the chilled air as she reached for the buttons that closed the front of her simple dress. It would not be a comfortable night, as she could hardly remove her stays and petticoats. Sleeping next to him in only her shift required an intimacy that did not yet exist between them—and likely never would.

Draping the thick kersey traveling dress over the

same chair with her cloak, she sat down on the bed to remove her boots.

"What the devil are you wearing?"

She gasped in shock as she glanced over her shoulder to see her husband staring at her. "You are not supposed to look."

"What sort of device have you harnessed yourself into?"

"They're stays."

"I've seen stays," he said. "I daresay I have a better acquaintance with ladies' undergarments than you do... and those are not stays. It looks some sort of medieval torture device!"

He wasn't wrong. Her father had insisted she wear such garments from the time she was a very young girl. He'd thought her figure too generous and insisted she looked vulgar, no matter how modest her dress. "They are restrictive but necessary."

THE STAYS in question were the most confounding item of clothing he'd ever seen. He'd yet to see his wife in anything that did not cover her from her chin to her ankles. There was never a hint of bare shoulders or décolletage, which suddenly made much more sense. Her stays covered her entirely, and they were laced so tightly that he could barely fathom how she breathed. In the wash-stand mirror, which allowed him to see the front of the garment, he could see that her breasts were completely flattened. The fabric was cutting into her skin in such a way that it could only be painful.

"Take it off," he insisted.

"It would be indecent," she protested.

"It's painful to look at! Good lord, woman! I've seen breasts before. I'll hardly fall on you like some ravening beast at the mere sight of them," he snapped. "Take that blasted thing off, or I will cut it off of you."

Mayville wasn't entirely certain what happened. One moment he was making only partially idle threats, and the next he was ducking flying footwear. She'd hurled her boot at him in a fit of a temper. Looking on incredulously, he saw that she held its companion in her hand and was brandishing it threateningly. "Are you mad?"

"Mad? Perhaps, but not insane. I've been bullied, belittled, and badgered my entire life! By my father and now by you!" she shouted. "I don't care if you don't like my clothes or my face or my hair or anything else about me. But I'll not be snapped at and threatened into silence and blind obedience."

His own temper flaring, Mayville rose and advanced toward her, closing the gap. As he rounded the bed, she let the other boot fly, and it struck his shoulder with a loud thud before falling to the floor. Weaponless, she faced him with her hands curled into claws, clearly ready to scratch his eyes out. Rather than give her the chance, he simply scooped her up, tossed her face down onto the bed and, with a simple flick of the knife he always carried in his boot, cut the laces on the offending garment.

All the while, she kicked and squirmed, shrieking at

him like a madwoman. Through the course of their strug-
gle, she managed to turn over so that they were facing one
another.

It didn't escape his notice that the position was
blatantly carnal, even if their current thoughts were not.
She was beneath him while his straddled her, pinning her
arms to the bed. And, against all odds and probabilities,
he found himself responding to her—*wanting her*. Bully,
he might be, but he was not a monster. Letting go of her,
he backed away instantly.

"Now, if you can be reasonable, we'll talk. No doubt
having adequate circulation to all parts of your body
should improve your disposition," he stated.

She did not have the anticipated reaction. He'd
thought it would spark her temper, that she would come
at him like some wild creature. Instead, she just stared at
him in horror. And then she began to sob. Not soft snif-
fles and pretty tears like other ladies of his acquaintance,
who still had a mind to their appearance. These were not
the tears of a woman who used them to manipulate.
These were the tears of a woman who had held them in
far too long. Great, gulping sobs wracked her body. The
tears streamed down her face unchecked as she drew her
knees up and hid her face against them.

"I'm not going to hurt you," he insisted, guilt gnawing
at him for having made her weep so. "But you cannot
wear such a thing. Whoever made you—"

He stopped there. He knew who had made her wear
it, just as he knew she'd likely faced bitter consequences
for any refusals to do so. Her father. And what had he

done? He'd been a bully and a brute, just as she'd accused him of. Instead of offering her an alternative, he'd simply manhandled her and acted like an arse.

It didn't last long. She managed to pull herself together and once more take control of her emotions. Such displays seemed out of character, though given what the last week had held for her, was it any wonder? From having a strange man sneak into her room, a forced wedding, and disownment by her father, only to now be the source of hateful gossip? She had every reason to cry.

"I didn't mean to hurt your feelings," he said softly, settling himself on the bed. "I'm not very good at this."

"At what?" she asked.

"Being a husband. Being a decent human being," he admitted. "I do not, as a rule, spend my time with very good people. Or kind people. I forget how they behave towards one another. I shouldn't have bullied you. Why on earth did he make you wear such a thing?"

She still hiccupped every so often, though the sobs faded. After a moment, she patted her cheeks to dry the tears there and said softly, "He said that my figure was unseemly and that it did not reflect well on a man of God to have a daughter whose appearance could only ever be described as vulgar and fast."

"I really hate him," he said. "I always did, just on principle, but now... When next I am in Boston Spa, I mean to plant him a facer that will send him sprawling into the dirt."

"It won't matter. You cannot undo what he has done," she said. "Knocking him down will only make more people whisper and gossip about me. I've been invisible all my life. It's very difficult to have people look at me now, whatever their reasons."

"You should not have to be invisible, but you shouldn't have to suffer the stares and whispers, either. All of this—contrary to what I may have said to be intentionally provoking before—is my doing. I have ruined us both, I fear. Now, take that blasted thing off and toss it into the fire. You'll have proper stays in the morning."

"Where on earth will you find stays in a crowded inn?"

"A bit of coin can talk many ladies out of far more than their stays," he replied with a grin. "Now go to sleep. You're beyond exhausted, and so am I."

CHAPTER SEVEN

The next morning, Althea awoke not only to new stays but to a lovely dress in a rich and vibrant shade of plum. They were draped over the chair in place of the ugly gray gown she'd worn for the first few days of their journey. The stays which had prompted their disagreement the night before were nowhere to be seen. Perhaps he'd made good on the threat to burn them.

Rising from the bed, she crossed to the chair and examined the pieces. Both garments were terribly fine, the fabrics luxurious and the stitching on each one a work of art. She'd never, not in the entirety of her life, owned something that was actually beautiful. *Until now.*

"Good morning."

Althea's head whipped around, and she found him seated before the fire in a straight-backed chair. He was already dressed, or mostly so. There was a small table there, laid with breakfast, and she hadn't even heard him enter.

"I must have slept like the dead," she mused.

"You did. And you snore. Not terribly loudly, but soft, little snuffling sounds," he teased. "Rather like a puppy."

Her eyebrow arched as she eyed him skeptically. "You are unnaturally cheerful today."

"I've had coffee. It's remarkable what that will do to improve one's mood. Would you like some? Or are you a tea drinker?"

"Tea," she admitted. "I've never had coffee."

"It can be an acquired taste," he admitted, pouring tea into one of the waiting cups for her. "Sit down and eat. Neither of us had supper last night, and I can only think that had something to do with my foul temper and your...emotional state."

"I had rather thought my emotional state was a direct result of your foul temper," she remarked. Recalling her own feelings of deep insecurity as she'd stood in the tap room and waited for him to get their room sorted, she sighed. "Though, that might be a slightly unfair assessment."

"Well, no more. I shall curb my temper, you shall refrain from throwing boots at me, and we shall attempt to get to London in one piece, with your wardrobe slightly improved in the process."

She glanced back at the traveling gown. "Where on earth did you find it?"

"Let's just break our fast and not focus too much on the previous owner of that garment. She's been fairly compensated for it, and that is all that should concern you about her."

A doxy. It was the only explanation. But another glance at the rich fabric and the beautiful color and she didn't care what the previous owner's occupation had been. She wanted to wear it. She wanted, even if only for the day, to not feel like the dowdy spinster she'd been forced to play throughout her adult life.

"You're right. It doesn't matter," she said.

SHE WAS WEARING ONLY her chemise and a bodiced petticoat. In truth, the garments were heavy enough that she was far more adequately covered than many ladies of *the Ton* were when they attended various balls. But the absence of the offending stays, which hid any hint of femininity in her figure, had created something he had not expected. It had created an awareness in him of what lurked beneath her dull, drab and utterly serviceable clothing. Recalling the way she'd felt beneath him, a familiar rush washed through him, making his blood surge.

Contrary to what her father might have said, her figure was anything but vulgar. It was, however, surprisingly lush and voluptuous in a way that he had not antici-pated—ways that made their current situation even more difficult. He had not reached a decision about her propo-sition, about siring a child for her followed by seeking their own separate lives. He didn't want this unforeseen desire for her to cloud his judgement on the matter.

Her hair, pulled into a single braid, was mussed from sleep. No longer scraped back into a tight and unforgiving chignon, the effect softened her features, revealing that same prettiness he'd spied in her when she'd been flushed with temper. Coupled with his newly discovered awareness of her other charms, he found himself doing the very last thing he'd ever wanted—lusting after his own wife.

She walked toward the small table where he was seated. He caught the faintest whiff of the simple scent she wore. It was only rosewater, but on her, the scent of it was far too tempting. He suddenly found himself wondering precisely where that scent was applied. It was a dangerous preoccupation.

There were scones on the table, glazed with sugar. She took a bite of one, and he could see the sugar glistening on her lip. The urge to taste it was so overwhelming, he gripped the table edge to keep from acting on it. Shaking his head to clear it of such thoughts, he knew he had to escape their chamber.

"Well, I'm going to the check with the coachman to be certain everything is prepared for the day. We should make London by the afternoon." Rising from his chair, he quickly made his way toward the door. It had been a noticeably hasty departure, but it was safer than the alternative.

At the bottom of the stairs, Mayville paused. It was very early morning, far too early for any respectable man to asking for hard liquor. And, yet, he was tempted. He was tempted to step into the taproom and ask the innkeeper for his finest whiskey. It had been easier to numb himself to everything, to ignore the young woman who was suddenly so entangled in his life, when he'd had the pleasant buzzing of heady spirits flowing through him. But, for three days, he'd not had a drink, save for wine with their dinner. And, for three days, he'd felt himself losing the apathy that he'd cultivated for nearly a decade and a half.

In the end, he did not step into the taproom. Instead, he stepped outside into the crisp air and made for the stables, where his coachman was preparing the carriage. There was naught for him to do; the man knew his job and did it well. It had simply been the only excuse for an escape that he could come up with in that moment.

"Women are the devil, Fredricks," he said as the man looked up.

The coachman grinned. "Aye. They are that, m'lord. But a finer road to hell, you'll never find."

CHAPTER EIGHT

Althea made her way down the stairs, with her cloak
draped over her arm. She hadn't been able to bear the
idea of covering the beautiful gown with that drab
garment. The new stays had required some adjustment.
Staring at herself in the mirror after she'd put them on,
she'd been mortified at how much of herself was still
displayed by them. Even with the gown over top of them,
the neckline was far lower than she was comfortable
with. She very much feared that she would spill out of it
the first time the carriage hit a rut in the road.

Despite being far more exposed than was typical for
her, Althea also felt something else. She felt pretty. The
last time she could remember feeling that way, she'd been
playing with some of the younger children from church.
The girls had asked to braid her hair. They'd plucked
wildflowers and woven them into the braids, creating a
floral crown for her. She'd thought it lovely...until her
father saw it. He'd ripped the flowers from her hair,

shoved her roughly to floor, and made her pray to be delivered from the sin of vanity. Meanwhile, he'd been corseting himself to fit into a satin waistcoat that he'd grown too fat for as he dined with his parishioners and demanded the choicest cuts of meat they had, due to his delicate constitution.

There had never been any illusions for her that her father was anything but a wicked man. However, while living with him and always being mindful to avoid his temper and his disapproval, it had been easy to ignore all the ways in which that wickedness manifested. It might have been a survival instinct, she supposed, rather like refraining from eye contact with a predator, who might see it as a challenge.

It was that thought which brought her to the man who was her husband. A dissolute rakehell who gambled, drank and, for lack of a better word, wenched. By all rights, he should have been wicked. He was certainly difficult, but he never intended harm, and when he did cause harm, he was very quick to apologize and quite sincerely.

All of it left her thoroughly befuddled. Shaking her head to clear it of all the riddles of confounding and difficult men, she stepped from the stairwell, onto the small area near the door. The taproom was on one side and the exit to the inn yard on the other. Not seeing Sinclair in the taproom, she exited through the door, into the clear, cold morning.

He was there, striding across the inn yard. He wore his waistcoat but hadn't bothered to tie his cravat. The neck of his shirt was open, as was his overcoat, as he strode toward her. He had not shaved, and the dark whiskers shadowing his jaw only highlighted the perfectly chiseled bone structure.

The last thing she'd needed to be reminded of was how handsome he was. It was something she was unlikely to forget.

"Your hair is different," he said as he neared her.

"I lost several hairpins last night." *When you threw me on the bed.* She didn't say it, but then again, she didn't have to. "I couldn't quite achieve my normal style without them."

"I like it this way," he said. "It suits you. Very fetching."

It shouldn't have mattered. It certainly should not have made her stomach flutter like a hundred butterflies were flitting about in it. But it did. Unable to meet his gaze, she ducked her head and murmured quietly, "Thank you."

There was a mere whisper of hesitation. And then she felt his hand beneath her chin, lifting her face with the slightest of pressure. "Do not hide. That is not how you live now. It's not who you are. It's only who he made you pretend to be."

Her heartbeat quickened. "I'm not sure I know how to be anything else, and I'm not sure I know how to respond to kindness from anyone, least of all you."

"I'm not certain it is kindness. I've little experience with receiving it or meting it out," he admitted. "Perhaps we can learn together...at least for a time."

"For a time," she agreed.

He stepped back, removing his hand from her face. "I'll see you to the carriage and retrieve our bags from the chamber. Then we'll be off."

"Everything is packed. It's on the chair before the fire," she offered.

He gave a curt nod before ushering her toward the waiting carriage and coachman. Once she was inside the conveyance, he turned back for the inn, leaving her to ponder that strange moment that had just passed between them.

A DRESS SHOULD NOT HAVE MADE SUCH a difference.

That thought crept unbidden to Mayville's mind for perhaps the hundredth time since they'd left the inn that morning. Of course, it wasn't simply the gown, really. It was the fact that he now had some inkling of what was hidden beneath it. And then there was her hair. No longer scraped back so tightly from her face, it softened her features and enhanced the rich, dark color of it. Deep brown, shot with hints of auburn and a true red, it was finally allowed to catch the light and display its brilliance.

They were nearing London, and it was later in the day than he would have liked. The roads had still been a muddied mess, and it had slowed their progress considerably. Still, they would arrive at his townhouse in Mayfair before teatime. His first order of business would be to send a note round to Gray, the Earl of Winburne, and his bride, Sabine, inviting them for dinner. He needed to have a buffer between them. Being alone with her, given his newly discovered attraction for her, was a dangerous prospect. There was still the matter of her proposition, after all. There were few people he would trust enough to discuss such a thing with or to seek their guidance. Winburne was perhaps the only one.

Across the expanse of the carriage, he could see her craning her neck to look out the smallish window. Taking pity on her and her curiosity, he raised the shade so that the weak afternoon light poured into the small space and gave her a better view of the city as they approached.

She blushed and looked away from him for a moment. "You must think me terribly gauche, but I've never been anywhere other than Boston Spa. I think I went to York once as a very small child, but I have no memory of it. I've never seen such things."

He glanced out the window himself then, trying to see it through her eyes. All he saw was dirt, poverty, and misery. But he didn't wish to curb her enthusiasm with his own pessimistic outlook. "I think your curiosity is natural, even endearing. It's rare in my world. Everyone I know is jaded and cynical."

She frowned at that, a small furrow forming between her brows as she clenched her hands together. "I've no wish to embarrass you. You need not take me into society. I can only imagine the awful things that would be said of me. No doubt, they would pale in comparison to what my father has uttered, but these people are your friends—"

"They are people I know," he corrected instantly. "Very few of them have the distinction of being called *friend*. I sent a note round to one man who does have that distinction and made arrangements that we may dine with him and his wife. You may already know them, in fact, or at least him. The Earl of Winburne."

She blinked owlishly. "Oh, well, yes, certainly I know him. He's been a great benefactor of the church and is very well acquainted with my father. No doubt he has already been apprised of everything that has occurred."

"Oh, most assuredly," Mayville agreed. "But not by your father. Lady Helena has no doubt written him already. She is his sister, after all."

"I hadn't realized. I never saw them together. But it is easy enough to see the resemblance now that you have told me."

"Poor Helena," he replied with a grin. "She would be devastated to hear it."

"Nonsense. The earl is a very handsome man," she protested. "And their similarity does not at all require that Lady Helena should not be both incredibly beautiful and incredibly feminine. I find her terrifying, of course."

He laughed at that. "Most of us do. Helena is a force to be reckoned with. Though, I daresay you have made a friend for life with her. She decided instantly that she liked you, and her loyalty is swift and fierce."

The buildings were growing closer and closer together and the sky growing dim with the congestion of coal smoke and the pollutants of the city. He watched her face for any hint of disappointment, but she didn't seem to see all of that. Her gaze was trained on a spot in the distance. St. Paul's, of course, with its majestic dome towering over everything around it. There was a wonderment in her expression that left him feeling unsettled and perhaps a bit ashamed of himself. There was so much he took for granted and simply accepted as his due.

They continued in silence, hers awestruck and his painfully introspective. He didn't speak until they turned onto Park Lane. "Hyde Park is a pleasant enough excursion if you time it correctly. Early in the day, it's all about putting oneself on parade. In the afternoon, such as it is now, it's all nursemaids and spoiled children."

"I would likely prefer that—and have more in common with the nurses and governesses than with the society misses," she answered with a laugh.

"You will like Sabine. And she will see to it that you are outfitted well enough that no one—in society or elsewhere—would ever dare insult you."

She shook her head. "They will dare. But I'll wear the fine clothes because I'm aware of how it would reflect on you if I did not. You may detest my father, and with very good reason, but he did teach that particular lesson very well. I know how important appearances are."

CHAPTER NINE

Althea awoke to the bustling of several maids striding into the room, each one carrying buckets of steaming water. One by one, they disappeared behind an ornate chinoiserie screen. They filed out of the room in the same manner, leaving only one of their ilk behind. The girl, dressed in a simple black gown with a white apron and white mob cap, bobbed a curtsy. "Your bath, my lady."

My lady. That was her, Althea realized. It was something she wasn't certain she'd ever grow used to. "Thank you...Sarah?"

The girl nodded. "Yes, ma'am. The Countess of Winburne will be arriving in just over an hour. She's to take you to her shop and get you properly outfitted today, per his lordship's instructions. His lordship said that, rather than dine here tonight, you will be dining with the Earl and Countess at their home."

The initial gut-clenching rebellion she felt at that pronouncement was quickly tamped down. No, he hadn't told her when they would address her wardrobe, but he had told her it would occur, and it only made sense to do so sooner rather than later. Perhaps the real issue was that the brief accord they'd reached after the debacle on the last night of their journey seemed to have made no lasting change in how they would get on. He'd avoided her entirely since they'd reached London. He'd brought her into his townhouse, introduced her to the servants, and promptly vanished.

She'd felt the pitying gazes of the footmen last night as each dish had been served to her, alone in the massive, formal dining room, wearing the only slightly formal gown she owned. It had looked shabby and out of place even to her. In turn, she had also appeared shabby and out of place.

Still, it wasn't the maid's fault that the man who was her husband could barely be bothered to speak to her. Pushing back the bedclothes, she rose and crossed the expanse of the room. The fire had already been built up. Even beneath her bare feet, the rug was soft, and when she stepped onto the wooden floor, there was no chill there to take her breath away.

The small luxuries, the things others took for granted, were the very things that made her aware of just how different her current life was from her prior one. Even with the humiliation of her husband's complete disinterest, no one was shouting at her. No one struck her when the floor wasn't scrubbed to perfection or when she dared to say something that was considered impertinent. There was no shouting—well, very little shouting. No one hurled insults at her and told her she was ugly and stupid, though there were moments when she certainly felt both of those things to the depths of her soul.

Make the best of it, Althea.

With those cautioning words reverberating in her mind, Althea stepped behind the screen, and the sight that greeted her made everything else vanish. The copper tub was large and deep. It was also full to brimming with water she had not heated and carried herself. Pleasant-smelling soaps rested in a silver dish on a small tray next to the tub, and drying cloths were draped carefully over a nearby chair. Even from a distance, she could see that they were soft and fine.

Whatever his reasons for allowing Rosedale to molder and ruin, they did not apply to the townhouse. Curious, Althea asked, "When did his lordship acquire this house, Sarah?"

"He bought it a few years ago, my lady, just before the previous Lord Mayville passed on. But he's not been here much in the past years. He keeps more in the north," the girl said.

He had purchased it. It had not been inherited from his father. It was a significant detail, Althea thought as she shed her night rail and stepped into the steaming tub of water. She hissed out a breath.

"Is it too hot, my lady?" Sarah asked, immediately concerned.

"It feels like heaven! Except, it feels so sinful, it surely cannot be," she admitted, sinking down into the water. All the aches and pains of the journey that she'd thought would simply linger for days seemed to dissipate in an instant.

Sarah made short work of washing and rinsing her hair. She then draped the mass of it over the edge of the tub and began combing it through so that it would dry before the fire.

Mindful not to get her hair in the water and undo all of Sarah's work, Althea washed carefully while the maid stepped out into the room and began readying her clothing for the day. She could hear the girl clucking disapprovingly at the sad state of her wardrobe. When even the servants found it lacking, there was certainly reason to worry.

Eventually, the water began to cool. No sooner had she acknowledged that sad fact before Sarah returned. She quickly looped Althea's hair into a loose knot and wrapped a cloth about it to hold it in place before spreading one of the larger drying cloths out for her.

Althea rose and wrapped the soft fabric about her before following Sarah out of the bathing nook and into her bedchamber proper. Laid out on the bed was the plum-colored traveling gown from the day before.

"It's not a day dress, my lady, I'm aware, but if you'll pardon me for saying, it's much finer than anything else and will be much easier to face down some of the folk what will be trying to get a look at you."

"Who would be trying to get a look at me?"

Sarah looked away, swallowing convulsively. "It were in the scandal sheets, my lady."

A feeling of dread washed through her. "What, precisely, was in the scandal sheets, Sarah?"

She turned fully away from her then, clearly feeling that simply avoiding eye contact was not enough of a separation when imparting such terrible news. "It's all over London that his lordship has taken a vicar's daughter to wife."

"That hardly seems worthy of such scandal and gossip. Sarah, you need not try to spare my feelings. I'd far prefer to have the unvarnished truth," Althea insisted.

The maid let out a terrible sigh, one tinged with deep regret. "They said you was a very plain vicar's daughter and hinted that perhaps you were some sort of adventuress, set off to catch a title by any means necessary. But you're not plain, even if you were made to dress plain. So, this gown will see that rumor put to rest, at least."

"I am actually rather plain. Not an adventuress. I cannot fathom how I can be both a plain spinster and some wicked female, intent on selfish gain through the use of my feminine wiles, all at the same time," Althea mused. "They have made it impossible to win in either direction. If I continue to dress drably, then I prove I am indeed plain and make everyone question what circumstances could have led to our marriage. If I remake myself into something more glamorous, more fitting with the image of the wife of a peer, then surely I am the adventuress all claim me to be."

The maid's lips firmed, and her eyes were flashing with righteous indignation. "They'll talk one way or another, my lady. I see no reason that you ought not to look nice while they do it. A pretty gown or two won't hurt a thing, and clearly his lordship is quite pleased to provide them for you."

Althea nodded. "You are quite right, Sarah. I won't be extravagant, but there is no reason that I should be an embarrassment to him when we go out. Let's do something with this hair, shall we?"

MAYVILLE WAS in his study when Sabine and Gray arrived. Sabine was shown to the drawing room to await Althea, while Gray closeted himself inside the masculine domain. There was no hesitation on the part of his oldest friend. Gray simply walked in, settled himself in the chair opposite him, and demanded, "What the devil happened?"

"A terrible lapse in judgement...and in my sense of direction," Mayville admitted.

"That results in getting lost. It does not result in getting oneself leg-shackled," Gray insisted. "She's not a bad sort. I've always found her very pleasant, if quiet and shy. Her father's a bit of an arse."

"More than a bit. He's an abusive bastard," Mayville replied. "Not that I have room to call anyone else's character into question. But it's done now. There is, however, another matter on which I would seek your counsel."

Gray steepled his hands and nodded. "Of course."

"I do not want a wife. I jested about pursuing Helena

just to make Blakemore miserable, but we both know I never would have."

"So, are you thinking divorce or annulment?"

"Neither," Mayville admitted. "My bride has offered a proposition. She will agree to completely separate lives, separate households. I will provide a generous allowance and will provide her with a child, and she will leave me alone to rot along with Rosedale Manor."

"That is what you want?" Gray demanded. "I know that you've taken this ridiculous vow to destroy all that your father and grandfather built, including Rosedale. But there is no reason, even if you want to let the house go to ruin, that you must go with it."

"I have been too many years on my own and too devoted to my many vices to make a good husband. And she is not inclined to like or trust men, something I cannot blame her for. It solves a problem and potentially leaves an heir to the title. While my father and grandfather deserve my disdain, their predecessors do not. There is no reason the title itself should fall into extinction," Mayville stated.

"Then, it sounds as if your decision is made."

"I suppose it is," he mused. "It's more a matter of asking something else. To this point, there has been no one else in my life who required looking after. If something were to happen to me, I should like to know that you would act as a trustee of sorts for her and the child, if there is one."

"You know that I would. But what on earth might

happen to you? You're not on the verge of doing something reckless, are you?"

"No. But we both know that I have enemies. I have made it a point to make them over the years, in fact. For once in my life, I'm electing to proceed with caution."

Gray shrugged. "Then, so far as I can tell, the vicar's daughter has had a remarkably positive effect on you. I hope you will consider not banishing her from your life."

"It will not be immediate. After all, we want gossip to die down, rather than be stirred to a frenzy. But we will part ways. No woman should have to tolerate the vagaries of my mood."

"You may find that having a wife will improve your mood sufficiently—if she is the correct wife."

Mayville laughed. "I would never be so lucky as to stumble, on accident no less, into the bedchamber of the one woman in all of England who could make it worth my while to reform myself. This is not a fairy story for children, my friend."

"Come. Let's go to the club and be certain that your lovely bride is not in the betting book. I'm not nearly so fond of dueling as you are."

CHAPTER TEN

Althea stood on a dais in the fitting room of Madame de Roussard's, dressed in only her chemise and stays. She'd never been in a modiste's shop before. She'd never actually had a garment made by a modiste. She'd sewn most of her own clothing, out of necessity, from patterns that were anything but fashionable. They'd never been anything but simple, serviceable, painfully modest garments.

"I think dark and rich colors for you," the Countess of Winburne said.

"Oh, yes!" Bridget, the shopgirl, agreed. "And simple garments. No ruffles or flounces. Well-made and well-fitted but with a very daring décolletage."

"Quite right," the countess agreed. "Get the silks in sapphire, crimson, and apricot. I want the indigo muslin, the block-printed cotton in red and white, and whatever else catches your eye."

"You cannot possible make so many dresses for me," Althea protested. "I should never need so many."

"My dear Lady Mayville," the countess said, "I know you think so. But this is not Boston Spa. And, in society, you cannot be seen wearing the same gown more than once. We will be economical and make overdresses and spencers that will alter the look of your garments so that you may get multiple uses from them, but rest assured when I say that you will need far more dresses than you could ever imagine. There is one particular dress that is already made up that I think I shall send home with you. It will require some alteration but not very much. You will wear it for dinner tonight. You must trust me when I say this, it is black, but the velvet will look marvelous against your skin, and I think it will suit your coloring far better than you might realize."

"I defer to your judgement, of course. I've no sense for fashion, as such a thing would never have been permitted to flourish in my father's house."

The countess frowned. "I know what it is to live in a house where one is not allowed to flourish. But I trust that Mayville is treating you well?"

"He is typically kind when in my presence, though that is rare. Most often, he is simply absent or indifferent," Althea replied.

"And is that what you wish for from him? Indifference or kindness? What of passion or love? I understand your marriage began under somewhat unusual circumstances. That does not necessarily mean it should continue in that fashion."

"It doesn't matter what I wish. He has no desire for a wife, and whether I could be the sort of woman he desires or not, it does not change that he wants something very different for himself," Althea protested.

"You will call me Sabine, and I shall call you Althea, and we shall be the best of friends. Female friendship is something I fear we are both lacking. And, in the spirit of friendship, I will tell you that I was very lucky to meet a man who knew precisely what he wanted, because, in my experience, very few of them do. Do not listen to what he says, Althea. Watch what he does. It will tell you much more about him than mere words ever could."

Althea looked away. Because all she could think of was the way she'd felt when he'd touched her face so gently the last morning of their journey. She still didn't know what had prompted it, and if Sabine was to be believed, perhaps he did not either. But those words had given her a traitorous hope, and she very much feared that would only lead her to bitter disappointment. It would be so much easier if he were truly a vile man. But, despite his drinking, despite the fact that she knew he gamed and wenched and fought numerous duels (moreso over cards than women), he wasn't a man to be reviled. There were many layers to him, and he was far more complicated than she could ever have realized when she only thought him so handsome it had rendered her mute in his presence.

"Will you think about what I've said? Please?" Sabine asked.

Althea nodded. "I will consider it. But I think he may be very certain of his mind."

"Time will tell, my dear. It always does."

———

THEY'D BEEN at the club for most of the day. He'd fielded countless well-wishes, some genuine and others less so, for the better part of the day. As a rule, Mayville disliked having so many people know his business, but as there was little recourse, he simply had to weather it. Of course, it hadn't all been convivial. There were those who held him in no small degree of contempt, those who had attempted to cheat him at cards or had attempted to cheat others in his presence. There was a great deal of resentment in those individuals, and they did not bother to hide their disdain. Luckily, however, neither his nor Althea's names appeared on the betting book. Any wagers about the nature or duration of their marriage were held privately.

Returning to Gray's home for their evening meal, Mayville was relieved to be finished with that chore. He'd gone, he'd confirmed, he'd endured the whispers and gossip, and now he could get on with the business at hand. He'd see his solicitor, make the necessary financial arrangements for Althea and any child they might have, consummate their marriage until such a time as she became with child, and then pack her off to some cozy, well-appointed estate in the south of England, where she could live in comfort and ease.

As they entered the house, the sound of feminine voices and soft laughter greeted them. "They appear to be getting on well enough," he observed.

Gray shook his head. "How have you seduced so many women, when you clearly know nothing about them? Women only talk and laugh that way when they are talking about and laughing at us. You're a bloody fool."

"Oh, I'm well aware. The different between us, my friend, is that I never assumed we would not be the topic of both their conversation and their derision," Mayville replied. "Shall we join them and curb their enjoyment at our expense?"

Gray gestured toward the drawing room door for Mayville to precede him. As they neared it, a footman stepped forward and opened the doors for them. Inside, the chatter and giggles immediately stopped. But as he entered the room, whatever snide comment had hovered on his lips faded into nothing. He was rendered quite speechless by the sight before him. Draped in a daring gown of black velvet, the neckline low and deep enough to reveal an ample amount of her generous bosom, Althea did not look like the woman he had married. She only slightly resembled the woman he'd seen leaving the White Hart in the morning before. This creature, with her artfully styled hair and fashionable dress, was a woman of beauty and mystery. Surely, he thought, clothes and a new hairstyle could not achieve so much!

"Doesn't she look splendid?" Sabine asked. "I knew that gown would be lovely on her."

Realizing that he'd been called upon to provide some sort of reply, Mayville managed to nod. "Yes. Yes, quite splendid. I hardly would have known you."

"As you hardly know me, I can't say that is a surprise," Althea replied with a bit of cheek. It wasn't mean, but it was certainly spirited.

"I believe the word you are looking for is *touché*, Mayville," Gray quipped.

He didn't care. The ribbing and good-natured teasing simply left him unfazed. The transformation in the woman who was now his wife—from dowdy spinster to sophisticated beauty—had left him so completely stunned that he didn't have the ability to think of anything else.

As he looked at her, he became aware of the fact that she had no jewelry. There were no flashing gems or pearls at her ears. Her only ornamentation was a simple gold cross on a thin chain about her neck. He hadn't even given her a ring, he realized. It was much worse than being remiss. His lack of attentiveness in that area was sending a very clear message to both Althea and everyone who encountered them that she wasn't truly his bride. And while he might harbor that feeling, he would not see either of them humiliated by having the whole of society discussing it. If they were to go about amongst other members of *the Ton* and not have her be a laughingstock, it was a matter he would have to rectify.

The dinner gong sounded then, jarring him from his thoughts.

"Just in time," Sabine said, sailing gracefully toward Gray, her skirts swishing slightly. She was all smiles for her husband.

Stepping forward, Mayville offered Althea his arm. "You do look lovely," he offered. "Please do not take my faint praise for an accurate reflection of your appearance."

"Sabine is magical. She can transform the proverbial sow's ear into a silk purse after all, it would seem," Althea remarked.

"Do not. Do not belittle yourself in that way. Her ability is to uncover a woman's beauty, not to fabricate it. This gown did not make you beautiful. But it did strip away the layers you've been hiding under that I might see it."

Her steps faltered, and she looked at him with such naked fear that it felt almost like a fist to the gut.

"Please do not say things to me that you do not mean. I am not part of this world, and I know that. Empty flattery may be considered polite conversation by ladies of your acquaintance—"

"Empty flattery is, quite often, meaningless conversation," he agreed. "But I do not engage in either. If I say something to you, Thea, I mean it. I am not the sort to spare your feelings. Heaven knows that. I've been naught but a brute and a bore since the moment we were wed."

"You haven't only been a brute and a bore," she replied softly. "You were also a bully. And sometimes—but only sometimes—you were even charming."

He was still grinning when they made their way to the dining room to join Gray and Sabine. In fact, he was grinning so hard that he missed the knowing look which passed between the other couple.

CHAPTER ELEVEN

It was very late when they returned home, but when they entered the townhouse, there was no great rush to part company. They walked slowly up the stairs together, until they reached the door to her chamber.

"Invite me in, Thea. There are things we need to discuss privately," he said.

"It is your house."

"It's *your* room," he countered. He would not push her or bully her as he'd done before.

With a hand that visibly trembled, she reached out and turned the knob to open her chamber door. She stepped over that threshold and paused for just a moment, before stepping aside and leaving the door open for him to follow.

Stepping inside, he closed the door softly and turned to face her. "It's about your proposition. Your desire to have a child."

"I thought it might be. You've made a decision, then?"

"I have," he said. "I agree to your terms. We shall consummate our marriage and remain together until you have a child. Then I shall procure a small estate somewhere in the south—Bath might be to your liking—where you may live comfortably with the child."

"Our child," she corrected. "Not *the* child. You may not wish to be a part of their life, but you will acknowledge them, I hope."

"Yes, of course. I did not mean to imply otherwise. But you must understand my need for distance in some ways. Whatever child we have, it will be much better off for not having me as a part of its day-to-day life. You do see that, don't you?"

She frowned. "I see that you believe it. I also see that when I lived in my father's house, I heard how stupid and ugly I was so many times that I believed it."

"No one is telling me that I am a terrible man who would make a terrible father, Thea. I am not being abused in that way," he replied.

"But you are," she answered. "And, perhaps saddest of all, you are doing it to yourself."

The accusation stung. It rattled him, and so he lashed out. "I'm not some broken thing to be repaired by you. I didn't need your father's brand of salvation, and I do not require yours, either."

Her lips curved in a mockery of a smile. "It is just as well. I wasn't offering salvation or redemption. Only observing. The type of salvation and redemption you require is something I cannot give you."

Goaded by his temper, he stepped forward and

caught her wrist, pulling her to him. It was a firm grip, but not bruising. She could have broken free of him if she wanted. But she did not. He could see that in her eyes. "You are so very pious, Thea. You stand in judgement of me because you do not know the pleasures to be had in wickedness."

"I do not judge you any more than you judge me. You think me plain and dull, pious and hypocritical. Before you stumbled into my bedchamber by mistake, you didn't even know I existed, because I was beneath your notice," she answered bitterly.

It was an accusation he couldn't deny. "I see you now. But the question, Thea, is whether or not you are ready for my attentions?"

He did not give her the chance to answer. Instead, he did the very thing that he had been so tempted to do since that night at the inn when he'd cut her ridiculous stays from her. He dipped his head, pressing his lips to hers.

Despite his piqued temper, it was a gentle kiss. The slings and arrows they seemed to throw at one another all the time did not extend to this particular use of their lips. Her response was hesitant, stilted—but it was a response and not a reluctant one. She hesitated out of uncertainty about the mechanics of kissing, not the desire to kiss and be kissed in return.

The temper that had sparked it faded into only a whisper of memory. Instead, he focused on that soft and gentle scent of roses that clung to her, on the delicate texture of her skin beneath his fingers, on the soft sighs and shuddering breaths that escaped her as the kiss continued. It grew, transforming into something that he did not recognize. Slow, languorous, alternately teasing and tender... It was still surprisingly chaste. Nothing more intimate than the gentle melding of their lips. But he wanted more, and he worried what might happen if he demanded it.

Still, instinct would not be denied. And the need to taste her more fully, to deepen that kiss until it mimicked the very carnal acts that he wanted to indulge in with her, it guided him more than thought ever would. When he slid his tongue gently over her bottom lip, she froze. But it was shock more than fear, he realized, as after a moment she settled against him.

That sort of innocence was something he couldn't even recall. It should have halted him, should have made him reconsider his current course. But it did not. He wasn't certain that anything existed in the world that could sway him in that moment. And so, he hauled her closer to him, wrapping his arms tightly about her until she let out a startled gasp. Then he swept his tongue between her parted lips, a gentle invasion that had her going stock-still against him. But only for a moment. Then, for lack of any better description, she simply melted against him. Her arms draped about his neck, and her breasts pressed against his chest until he could feel the hardened buds of her nipples. Then his hands were sliding over the elegant black velvet gown, down to her hips then to the lush curve of her bottom, pressing her against him so intimately that even the most innocent of misses would be unable to mistake his desire.

Reaching for the simple lacing at the back of her dress, he loosened the tapes there until he could tug the short velvet sleeves off her shoulders, the bodice slipping low enough to reveal the upper swells of her breasts. Only then did he pull his lips from hers. Immediately, he began to kiss the curve of her jaw, the long and slender line of her neck, her collar bone. But every kiss was calculated and measured to sweep her away, to ignite her passion to such a fever pitch that when he stripped that gown from her entirely, she'd never think to protest in maidenly shyness.

It was proving to be both an efficient and effective strategy.

Until her maid walked in.

THE MAID'S startled shriek brought Althea firmly down to earth. She was no longer floating on a cloud of bliss as the man she'd secretly longed for most of her life kissed her senseless. Instead, she was scrambling to back away from him and tugging her dress to rights as she did so.

She dared glance back at him, and what she saw had her cursing him and the maid. Naked hunger burned in his gaze. He watched her like a predator, his eyes never leaving her as he took in every detail, from her mussed hair and kiss-swollen lips to the fact that her breathing was far from even.

"Sarah, thank you, but I...I do not need assistance tonight," she stammered.

"Yes, m'lady. My apologies, my lady, my lord," the girl mumbled and then beat a hasty retreat.

As the door clicked closed behind her, Althea dared to face him directly. "What are you doing?"

"You want a child, Thea. Even for your puritanical sensibilities, I refuse to approach carnal acts as a drudging chore. Our bodies were made for pleasure, after all."

She shivered at the promise in his voice. "I was not expecting that."

He smirked. "I daresay there are many aspects of lovemaking that you will be surprised by. I look forward to introducing you to all of them."

"I'm not ready," she said.

"I'm aware. I never anticipated that I would take your virginity tonight, Thea. But I had thought, if you'd let me, that I would show you the pleasure you are capable of."

If not for the interruption, it wouldn't have even been a question. Had Sarah not entered the room when she did, Althea had little doubt that he would have had her naked and doing all manner of wicked things. But they had been interrupted. The haze of pleasure induced by that kiss had lifted long enough for doubt and fear to return. "I can't think. We go from snapping at one another to-to..."

"Kissing," he supplied. "You can say it without going to hell."

"That was not merely a kiss," she said. "It was a seduction, and we both know it."

"I had not planned it to be. There was no great plot afoot, Thea. That is not how I live my life. Planning things is for other people."

"I need time to think, to acclimate to this change in our relationship."

"The change you asked for," he reminded her. "I cannot make the act less pleasurable... Well, I could, but it goes against all reason to do so."

She shook her head. "I'm not asking you to make it less so. I'm asking you to give me a moment to think about it, to digest it all."

"You have until tomorrow night...but only if I get to kiss you again," he offered.

"That isn't fair!"

He stepped forward, sweeping her into his arms once again. "Life rarely is."

Those words were still ringing in the air when his lips settled on hers once more. If the first kiss had been gentle, this was anything but. Hard, hungry, demanding. It robbed her of breath and left her incapable of thought. He stroked his tongue over her lips, sliding it between them in a blatantly carnal manner that left her reeling. Even more so, she returned that kiss, stroke for stroke. He commanded her, she realized. Her mind had no say in the matter, for her body simply swayed to his will. Like the snake charmers of India, he had found the tune that mesmerized her and left her pliant to his control.

When he let her go, it was so abrupt that she stumbled. But he was simply gone. He'd strode quickly toward the door and into the corridor beyond. A moment later, she heard another door slamming, and she sank to the floor on her knees.

"He will destroy me," she murmured. "And I will let him."

CHAPTER TWELVE

Mayville awoke naked in his own bed, very much alone. He hadn't even drunk himself into oblivion, a decision he'd regretted through much of the night as he'd lain there in a permanently aroused state. Rock hard and aching for the touch of his virginal wife until the wee hours of the morning when sleep had finally claimed him, he'd cursed her and himself for every kind of fool imaginable. Time, she'd asked for. Christ above, if he had to endure the torture of another night like the one before, she'd be a widow before ever being relieved of the burden of her innocence.

Pushing back the covers, he rose and stood beside the bed for a moment, contemplating the many contradictions of his wife. *His wife.* How easily he had accepted her in that role, he mused. Perhaps, in part, because he'd never imagined anyone else in it. Not for many years, at any rate. Not since Charlotte.

Her name crept into his memory and, as it always

did, cast a pall over him. It had been a decade since she'd married another, a decade since he'd discovered he was not truly fit to be anyone's husband, given the dark and ugly secrets he'd inherited. By now, she would know he was in town. She would also have heard that he'd taken a wife. It could complicate matters when he introduced Althea into society. Charlotte wielded a great deal of influence amongst *the Ton*. She could ease Althea's way, or she could make it impossible, if she chose to.

Striding purposefully toward the washstand, he splashed water on his face to clear the cobwebs of his sleepless night and then began dressing. His valet would no doubt be terribly put out, but he'd never been the slave to fashion that other gentleman of his ilk were. It was an unnecessary use of his time to belabor which knot would be best for his neckcloth on any given day.

Dressed simply in breeches, boots, and a dark waistcoat over his white shirt, he tied his neckcloth in a simple knot and donned his overcoat. He would ride in the park that morning and see what he could discover about Charlotte's whereabouts and her current frame of mind.

During their last meeting, when she'd sought him out to ask for his assistance with her brother and his less-than-above-board dealings with Lawrence Russell, things had been said that could make his current situation very difficult.

As he opened his bedchamber door to step out into the corridor, his valet was standing there looking utterly dismayed at finding him dressed. Ignoring the man's disappointment, Mayville said, "Inform Lady Mayville that I will be out for most of the day."

"But she has gone, my lord."

His stomach sank. "Gone?"

"Yes, my lord. The Countess of Winburne arrived early this morning and swept her away. I believe they have gone shopping."

"Oh," he said, inordinately relieved. When he'd heard that she'd gone, his first thought had been to interpret it as a more permanent sort of absence. "Then, should she arrive home before I do, you may inform her then, Dutton."

"Your hat, my lord?" The valet reminded him gently.

"It can hang," he snapped.

Leaving the valet sputtering behind him, Mayville headed for the stables. He'd see to his own mount. It would be quicker.

THE SHOPS on Bond Street were filled with ladies and their maids. As she perused the wares, eyeing delicately embroidered stockings and lovely, colorful garters, Althea could feel their curious gazes on her.

"You're doing wonderfully, you know?"

Althea glanced at Sabine, who stood at her side. "I feel like some sort of caged beast in a menagerie."

"It's an apt description. But, as someone who weathered a great deal of gossip, I can assure you it does fade quickly. The viperous ladies of *the Ton* are as fickle and flighty as they are vicious. Another scandal will come along. It always does," Sabine offered reassuringly. "In the meantime, you are a newly married woman, and your underpinnings and nightwear should reflect that. If I catch you looking at anything even remotely sturdy or serviceable instead of beautiful and seductive, I shall be very cross."

Althea couldn't help but smile at her teasing tone. When the time came for her to depart London and leave Sinclair behind, she would miss Sabine and the Earl of Winburne. They were perhaps the first friends she'd ever known. But she felt compelled to confess the truth to her. "It isn't like that with us. Not...well, not yet."

Sabine's eyebrows lifted in surprise. "You mean that you haven't—that is to say—"

"No. At first, he wasn't certain we would stay married. There was a great deal of talk about annulments in the beginning. But, well, I've made him an offer of sorts. That, if we have a child, we may live separately, and he can do as he pleases," Althea explained in a halting whisper.

"Is that truly what you want?" Sabine's concern was palpable.

"It is better than the alternative, I think. To live with him and know that he would rather I were anywhere else. I didn't ask for any of this, but the truth is neither did he. It was all a terrible misunderstanding, and now we are paying the price for it."

"Do you know, Althea, that last night was the first time I have seen him when he is not deeply in his cups,"

Sabine admitted. "I adore him. He's charming and wicked, and yet he is a true friend to Gray and to me. His assistance with my late husband was invaluable. Were it not for him, I doubt that Gray and I would be where we are now. I might have run out of fear. I think you could be very good for him, and I think, given what you've shared and what you haven't shared about your life in Boston Spa, perhaps he could be good for you."

Althea became aware then that the shop had grown terribly quiet. Looking up, she realized that all eyes were no longer on her. They were glued to the ridiculously beautiful woman who had just entered the shop. With startlingly blonde hair piled in a riot of curls atop her head, that cascaded gently onto her forehead to frame her piercing blue eyes, she was striking. The delicacy of her features was almost doll-like, except for her very full lips, which had to be rouged. No woman had lips the color of cherries, regardless of what bards and troubadours might say.

"Who is she?"

"Her name is Charlotte Farraday, Lady Bruxton. She was Miss Charlotte Hill before she married," Sabine answered.

"Is that supposed to mean something to me?" Althea asked.

Sabine looked at her with what could only be described as pity. "Many years ago, she was betrothed to Mayville."

Althea looked back at the woman who had drawn every eye as if it were her due. "Oh. I see."

The woman approached them, her full, red lips curved in a patently false smile. "Countess! How lovely to see you again! And how strange it is to think that when last we met, I was coming to you to have my dresses made."

"I still have a shop, Lady Bruxton, and we still produce the finest gowns in London," Sabine said, making no apology for her past or current affiliation with trade.

The false smile never faltered. "Naturally. But I cannot only frequent one shop. When so many ladies in society look to me for guidance and inspiration, it would be terribly unfair of me not to provide other shops with equal attention, wouldn't it?" The last was addressed directly to Althea. "I do not believe we've met."

"Lady Bruxton, may I present to you Althea Wortham, Lady Mayville. Althea, Lady Bruxton," Sabine introduced them reluctantly.

"Mayville?" Lady Bruxton repeated. "How utterly delicious. Where is your wicked husband, then?"

"I would presume he is at home," Althea replied carefully.

"You would presume? My dear, one should always know where one's husband is," the woman replied with a tittering laugh.

"Yes, well, he was sleeping when I left for the morning, and we did not have an opportunity to discuss his plans for the day," Althea replied.

Lady Bruxton's gaze hardened. "I see."

"We should go, Lady Mayville. I find there is little enough in this store to tempt me," Sabine inserted.

"Indeed. I shall inform my husband of our introduction, Lady Bruxton."

Lady Bruxton's smile tightened, giving the impression of a grimace. "You do that, my dear Lady Mayville. No doubt he will find it quite interesting, indeed!"

Once outside the shop, Sabine began to laugh. "Oh, dear heavens. The look on her face when you told her you'd left him sleeping... She was positively green with envy. You do understand what you implied with that statement, don't you?"

"I understand perfectly...in theory," Althea replied. "She's very beautiful, isn't she?"

"Like a piece of fruit rotting from the inside out," Sabine answered, linking her arm with Althea's. "But she's not your problem. She has a husband, and he is very, very rich. She will never leave him, and Mayville would never settle for being her lover."

CHAPTER THIRTEEN

They dined at home that evening, and not in the large, formal dining room. In the sitting room that flanked her bedchamber, a small repast had been laid for them. Of course, Althea understood its purpose. There were several bottles of wine laid out for them, and the table had been laid with beautiful China and silver, while roses from the hothouse were stationed at various intervals around the room. It was a scene set for seduction.

"This was quite a nice surprise," he remarked.

"Shall I congratulate you on it, Sinclair? It is a bit obvious, of course, but still lovely. Thank you for the effort," Althea replied.

He blinked at her. "I didn't do this. I thought you did."

"Well, who— Ah, Sabine," Althea deduced. "No doubt she sent instructions on my behalf. She is rather concerned that we have not had a proper honeymoon."

"We've not had a proper wedding night, either," he pointed out. "Do you suppose that is about to change?"

"I think it has to," she answered. "By the way, I met Lady Bruxton today. I understand you were once betrothed to her."

He choked on the wine he'd just sipped. "Christ," he muttered after he'd regained his breath. "Are you aiming for widowhood?"

"I'm certain her curiosity about me was only natural, all things considered. I might have liked to know of her existence beforehand, however. It was a rather unpleasant scene to run into your former ladylove while browsing stockings and other items in a shop."

"It only occurred to me this morning that it might be a problem," he explained. "I intended to see her and smooth things over—"

"There is naught to smooth over," Althea replied. "She is married to someone else, and for the time being, so are you."

"We have remained friendly," he reasoned. "I've assisted her with some private family issues in the past."

Althea dropped her gaze to the plate before her, the delicious food now tasting like sawdust in her mouth. "And are you still lovers?"

He was silent for a moment then said, "No. We are not. I will not deny that, for a very long while after she married Bruxton, I continued to have feelings for her. But there is nothing improper in my dealings with her."

"But she wishes otherwise."

"Yes. She has expressed that she would like to resume

our relationship, but I cannot. It is one thing to dally with a married woman when it is just a dalliance."

"But you love her."

"Loved," he admitted. "We were little better than children then. I daresay the last dozen years has changed us both dramatically. We are practically strangers, with only a shared past between us. But I've no wish to discuss Charlotte with you. Not tonight. Tonight was supposed to be for other things, Thea. Tonight was supposed to be for us, was it not?"

Althea looked up, ready to refuse him. After all, how could any man who had once loved a woman as beautiful as Lady Bruxton ever look at her as anything to be desired? Yet when her gaze met his, she saw his desire. It burned in his gaze, and under his regard she could feel an answering heat building inside her. She didn't answer, but she supposed it had been a rhetorical question, regardless. He was already out of his chair and walking around the small table, toward her.

"Dinner," he said, "can wait. This cannot, else you'll find some reason for us to argue again."

Althea allowed him to take her hand and lead her away from the table, toward the door connecting the sitting room to her bedchamber. He was not the sort to wait for her maid to come and ready her for bed, for her to don some night rail that would preserve her modesty. She rather feared modesty would not be permitted at all.

Following him into her bedchamber, she jumped when she heard the snick of the door closing behind them. But she wasn't given any time to consider what was about to take place. Almost instantly, he'd pulled her into his arms. The firm press of his body against hers, just as it had done the night before, robbed her of both speech and thought. Then his lips were on hers, offering the same sweet torment as before. But this time it was expected, and she simply gave herself up to it. The pleasure of it all, the ability he had to simply sweep her away... Those were unexpected. But it was what she had asked him for, after all. In order to have a child, they would have to consummate their relationship, and he was certainly the expert in that matter.

Once again, just as he'd done the night before, the laces of her gown offered little impediment to his questing fingers. But he didn't stop at simply drawing it from her shoulders. This time, she felt the fabric sliding over her arms, the bodice drooping and then the weight of the skirts simply pulling the garment down entirely until puddled at her feet. In all that, he never stopped kissing her, be it her lips or her neck and shoulders. His mouth was everywhere. The heat of it on her skin was like a brand.

When her stays simply vanished, the laces having been dealt with in an extremely skilled and clandestine fashion, she didn't protest. Her petticoat fell next, joining the gown on the floor. And then she wore only her chemise, stockings, and garters, plus the heeled slippers that had been purchased to compliment the dark-crimson gown she'd worn.

He drew back from her then, his gaze sweeping over her, taking in the gauzy and delicately embroidered chemise with its lace accents and the clocked stockings with their scarlet embroidery. "I see Sabine has been busy with your wardrobe... Remind me to thank her profusely."

Althea didn't reply as he'd simply taken her shoulders and turned her around so that her back was pressed to his chest. She could feel him plucking the various pins from her hair until the mass of it simply fell, cascading over her shoulders. When not contained, the unruly waves fell nearly to her waist.

He lifted one heavy strand, letting it slide through his fingers. "I had thought it was a crime to hide your lovely breasts. Had I known that your simple and severe hairstyles were concealing this sort of beauty... For shame, Thea."

"It's terribly inconvenient and always in the way when I am seeing to chores," she replied softly.

"And what chores do you have now?" he asked, his hands sliding under her hair to cup her shoulders before his fingers trailed down her arms to link with hers. "Planning menus? Discussing what silver to polish on any given day of the week?"

It was true. She was no longer scrubbing floors and beating rugs. Nor was she elbow deep in a laundry tub filled with harsh soaps that all but burned her skin. That terrible part of her life was now behind her.

She felt him move again, felt his lips slide just beneath her ear to kiss the tender skin there. It was instinct to tilt her head to the side, to give him greater access. Her eyes fluttered closed as she felt his tongue drift lazily over her skin, only to be followed by the slight sting when he scraped his teeth gently over that same spot. It left her shivering against him, both eager and terrified of what would come next.

"Do not fear me, Thea," he whispered against her ear. "Do not fear this. It is the most natural thing in the world."

"That is easily said when one has done it before. Falling down is natural as well, yet I dislike it very much."

He chuckled, his breath fanning over her heated skin. "Sometimes falling is the best part."

Before she could ask what he meant, he'd simply lifted her into his arms and strode toward the bed. He didn't place her gently on it. Instead, he tossed her into the middle of it with enough force that she bounced. A startled laugh escaped her, and then it transformed into a peal of giggles. It had been thoroughly unexpected that he would be playful, that he would make the experience *fun*. Passionate, yes. Pleasurable, certainly. But light-hearted and fun? She had not expected that at all.

But her laughter faded away as she saw him shrug out of his coat. His cravat and waistcoat followed. And as he pulled his shirt free of his breeches, bunching the fabric up to pull it over his head, she was treated to her first real sight of his body since the night he'd snuck into her room —the night she'd been too stunned to really appreciate what she was seeing.

He might have lived a dissolute lifestyle, but he managed to keep himself very fit in spite of it. This was not a man who needed corsetry or a skilled tailor to make his clothing look good. Not in the least. He was all firm, lean muscle and golden skin dusted with the lightest bit of burnished golden hair. Slightly thicker over his chest, it narrowed to a thin line that arrowed down the lean muscles of his stomach and disappeared behind the fall of his breeches.

Althea swallowed convulsively as she stared at him. He was like a work of art, really. She felt terribly ordinary in comparison, but he could well have been carved from marble by the masters of old.

When he climbed onto the bed with her, the length of his body pressed against her, thoughts of ancient art and doubts about her own appeal simply fled. They were replaced with only appreciation for the heat and firmness of him against her, for his hands as the roamed over her body, unerringly finding all the placed that would make her pulse race and her blood sing. And just as he'd said, it was the most natural thing in the world. She wrapped her arms about him, welcoming him, inviting him to take all that he wished from her.

CHAPTER FOURTEEN

If anyone had told him that the plainly dressed vicar's daughter would be such a passionate creature, he would have thought them mad. There was shyness, yes, but also eagerness and a willingness to be guided that left him trembling as he battled his own need for her.

Above all things, he would make the night pleasurable for her. He would allow her to see what passion and desire could truly make one feel. With that thought uppermost in mind, he placed one hand over the lush curve of her breast. The softness of that flesh, the weight of it in his hand, ratcheted his own need to a torturous level, but still he ignored it. Instead, he dragged the pad of his thumb over the hardened peak of her nipple and was rewarded with a shattered moan from her.

He repeated the gesture, each touch slightly different, each one driving her farther along that path to true completion. But when he dipped his head and took that pebbled bud into his mouth, her hands delved into his hair, holding him to her as she cried out. It was a moment of perfection for him, a moment that would be committed to memory for all time. Was there any greater victory in all his wretched life than to bring an innocent beauty to the fruition of passion and pleasure?

With that thought upper most in his mind, he continued to lavish attention on her sensitive nipples—laving with his tongue, nipping with his teeth—and as he did so, he began to slide his hand over her hips, along the long line of her thigh. He stroked her flesh with gentle persuasion until he could slip his hand between her thighs.

She stiffened beneath him, but only for a second. Then she took a deep, shuddering breath and parted for him, welcoming him.

He brushed the dark curls there, gently coaxing a response from her. And when she let out a broken sigh, only then did he slip one finger between the folds of her sex. The wet heat that greeted him had him gritting his teeth even as he stroked her tender flesh. Finding the small, taut nub that would quickly bring her to release, he watched her every response to determine what it was that she needed. Speed, intensity, the firm-ness or gentleness of his touch—he tailored it to her response, and the reward was her body straining beneath him, her thighs trembling as the pressure built within her.

"What are you doing to me?" she asked, her voice hoarse and breathless as she arched against him.

"You'll know soon enough," he whispered hotly. And

then he moved down the bed to press a kiss against the seam of her sex, inhaling her scent.

She let out a startled gasp, but it soon turned into a throaty moan as he pressed his tongue against her.

The taste of her was exquisite beyond his wildest imaginings. And he was so hungry for her that, even when he felt her shuddering with a violent release, he didn't stop. He drove her up and over that peak again and again, reveling in her unfettered response to him as she sobbed his name brokenly.

Only when she had collapsed bonelessly against the mattress did he lever himself up so that his body was pressed between her thighs. He could feel the heat of her against him through the fabric of his breeches. Fumbling with the buttons, as the fabric was stretched taut over his erection, he finally managed to free himself from the constricting garment. Fitting himself against her, he pressed in swiftly, piercing the barrier of her innocence with one sharp thrust.

She didn't cry out, but she did tense beneath him, her fingers digging into his shoulders so that he could feel the bite of her nails on his skin. He stilled against her, waiting for that pain to pass. And when she relaxed again, when the tension fled her muscles and she looked up at him without the haze of pain in her eyes, only then did he begin to move. Slowly, gently, with short and shallow strokes, he moved within her. And then her eyelids fluttered closed, her back arched, and she gave herself up once more to the pleasure he was stirring inside of her.

He found the strength of will, somehow, to maintain

that rhythm until he felt her shuddering with pleasure once more. The clutch of her heated flesh around him was more than he could bear, however. Thrusting deep one last time, he let his release wash through him, spilling himself inside her. And his only thought was that he hoped he did not get her with child. Not immediately. That was the sort of pleasure he would not readily give up for some time. The longer it took to give her what she wanted, the longer he could keep her for himself.

ALTHEA AWOKE TO AN EMPTY ROOM. It was still dark, the curtains still drawn at the windows, but the fire had recently been stoked and blazed cheerily in the hearth. Reaching out, she touched the bed beside her and found it still warm. A noise from the sitting room prompted her to look up, and then he appeared in the doorway, wearing only his breeches. In one hand he carried a glass of wine and in another a plate laden with bread and cheese, left over from their light supper.

"I worked up an appetite," he offered with a grin. "I imagine you did as well."

She couldn't stop the blush from stealing into her cheeks any more than she could halt the rumbling of her stomach in response to his question. She had indeed worked up an appetite. "I'm famished."

He crossed the room to the bed and sat the plate between them. "It's a very good thing, then, that I'm of a mind to share."

"I thought you'd gone," she admitted.

"I considered it," he said. "You are too tempting, and you are not used to the demands and rigors of a night like the one we've just shared. Every time I look at you, I want you again, but it's too soon for you."

He'd made love to her twice already. And if she were completely honest, she was sore. Her body ached from their exertions, but she'd gladly suffer that and more for the pleasure that he promised. Ducking her head, she looked away, embarrassed to acknowledge her own wantonness.

As if he'd peered into her mind to know that thought, he reached out to lift her chin with his thumb and forefinger, forcing her to meet his gaze. "There is no shame in what we have done, not in the act or in your pleasure in it."

"That is not what I have always been told. Women should not—"

"Should not listen to those who tell them their own bodies are wicked or sinful," he interrupted. "No doubt this was more wisdom imparted by your worthless father."

"It was," she admitted.

"Thea, I am not a religious man. In fact, I am as far from it as any man can be. I'm not even certain that I believe God exists," he offered, his voice soft and low. "But if he does, and if he made us in his own perfect image, then there is nothing about what our bodies are capable of that can be wrong. Our bodies are made to find pleasure in this act and, within the confines of marriage, there is no shame or sin in it. Anyone who says differently does so for their own purposes. Your father chose to humiliate and torment you at every turn. I cannot imagine that this was any different: a way to keep you under his thumb and prevent your being tempted to marry and leave him without a target for his abuse."

"I hate him," she admitted. "I have hated him all my life. But there was nowhere to go. He made certain that I would never have any offers of marriage. There was no escape. I often think that my mother died simply to get away from him."

"Whatever happens between us, you will never have to go back there. I make very few promises in my life, but that is one I offer freely, and it will be kept. Now, eat something, and we'll see if perhaps I can't find some creative way to make love to you that won't result in you not being able to walk tomorrow."

She had no interest in food suddenly. "It would be a small enough price to pay."

His eyes flashed even in the dim light from the fire. Without hesitation, he moved the plate to the table beside the bed and then pushed her back against the pillows. "In that case, we should indulge ourselves fully."

CHAPTER FIFTEEN

Entering the breakfast room, Althea noted that her husband was already present. Dressed in riding clothes, she could surmise from his damp hair that he'd already returned from his morning jaunt through Hyde Park.

"Good morning, Thea. You look rested," he teased.

She most assuredly did not look rested. It had been nearly two weeks since the first night he'd come to her bad. He'd been in it every night since and had done things that brought her to blush just thinking of them. Still, they'd managed to avoid further clashes of temper and had even begun, she thought, to form a sort of friendship, at least when she wasn't awestruck by him. It was also very dangerous ground. Liking him could lead to loving him, and loving him would only lead to disaster. Despite that, she was reluctant to disrupt the easy peace they had found with one another. So, she replied with a softly spoken, "Good morning, Sinclair."

"We've received the first round of invitations, it seems," he stated, switching to more serious matters. "The winter is upon us, and the Season has begun in earnest. Do not feel that you must accept every invitation that comes along. Choose the ones you are interested in, and then we will decide together which of those to attend. One or two per week should suffice."

Filling her plate at the sideboard, Althea paused to also grab the stack of correspondence that had been placed discreetly on a silver salver there. As she settled herself at the table, she began sorting through the missives one by one. "There is a musicale at the Forsythes. They are friends of yours, are they not?"

"They are. How did you know?"

"I recall them stopping in Boston Spa. When they toured the church, it was mentioned that they had acquaintances in the area," she said. *And any mention of him had prompted me to hang on their every word.*

He sighed. "Yes, they are friends, and yes, we should attend, although I'd rather eat that bloody invitation. Their daughters are entering society this year, and they are...lovely girls but not at all musical. I expect it shall be a painful evening."

"What will happen when we see Lady Bruxton at events? I know you do not think it is a problem, but everyone in society is aware of your history and of the circumstances that led to our marriage. There will be whispers," she said. The gossip sheets were rife with all the same horrid stories her father had spread about them in Boston Spa. That gossip had followed them to

London and would not go away any time soon, it seemed.

He sighed heavily. "Charlotte is not a problem. We have remained friendly over the years, but if we encounter her socially, we shall be cordial and move on. Do not allow the prospect of encountering her to make this more of a chore than it needs to be."

That dismissal stung. What did he mean by it? Was discussing their plans with her the chore? Or was it something more? Was being with her at all, in any capacity, the chore? She didn't know the answer, and she was beyond terrified to ask for clarification.

The newfound intimacy of their relationship had taken all those old feelings she had for him, the ridiculous school-girl crush that had no basis on the reality of who he was, and it had amplified those feelings until it was a wonder she could string two words together in his presence.

Rather than address it, she simply nodded. "Of course. I'm certain I'm worried about nothing. No doubt she moves in very rarified company, indeed."

Continuing the morning chore of sorting through the correspondence, when she reached the last one, her heart sank. The heavy vellum was folded with precision. And the red wax seal on the back was emblazoned with a heavily stylized letter B. Breaking the seal, her worst fears were realized. "I spoke too soon. Lady Bruxton is hosting a ball in our honor. In two weeks, we are to attend at their home on Upper Brook Street so that she may formally wish us well in front of everyone."

He blinked at that. But then his expression quickly shuttered. "It's quite an overture of friendship...and an excellent way to put an end to ugly gossip. You should accept with our gratitude."

"I shall write to her at once," Althea said. She looked at the plate before her, laden with the rich and heavy breakfast foods she normally adored. "I must be overly tired, I think. Food is no longer appealing to me. I shall see to the correspondence and then have a lie down. Good day, Sinclair."

"Yes, I'll be out for most of the day, Thea. You should rest. I'll be going for another ride, I think. Too many of the horses have been neglected of late. I'll be at the club till late."

She didn't answer beyond a simple nod of acknowledgement.

AN HOUR LATER, Mayville was in the park. He'd ridden back and forth along Rotten Row so many times he ought to have been dizzy. He was ready to give up and make for his club when he saw her. Charlotte, in her military-inspired riding regalia, was riding a great black beast of a horse. She cut quite a figure and knew it. She loved to be shocking. She always had.

He knew the moment she saw him. Her shoulders straightened, her chin lifted, and she offered him a victorious smile as she nudged her horse into a soft cantor.

When she finally reached him, she drew up abruptly, the horse rearing. It had been a practiced maneuver, designed to make everyone look in their direction.

"The subtlety of a cannon," he mused.

"Good afternoon, Sinclair. You have yet to call on me. I was so hoping you and your plain little bride would come for tea, I had to resort to drastic measures to get your attention," she replied.

"Do not speak of her," he snapped. "She is not like you—or me, for that matter. Thea is a decent person, good and kind. Far kinder than I deserve."

Charlotte gaped at him. "Are you falling in love with your little mouse, Sinclair? What a story that would be! And terribly ironic, since my husband will not live out the season. Here you are, married to a woman you could never truly want, all while I hover on the brink of freedom."

Her conceit was astounding. Had it always been so? Yes, he realized. Even when they'd been younger, when he'd been blinded by her beauty, he'd known her vanity was excessive. But her position in society, being toadied to by everyone else, had only made it worse. By God, she frustrated him. How had he ever thought himself in love with her? "I am not casting her aside for you," he stated emphatically. "And if that is true, if your husband truly is at death's door, shouldn't you be with him instead of here vying for attention?"

"Oh, he doesn't want me there. I'm useless in the sick room." She brushed at an imaginary piece of lint on her sleeve as she spoke. "Besides, riding helps me think. And I have so much to do to plan the perfect ball to welcome you and your mouse back to London society."

"Do not think to hurt her, Charlotte," he warned, "or you will regret it. I have enough information about your family to ruin you."

She blinked in shock. "Are you blackmailing me, Sinclair?"

"I'm warning you that actions have consequences and reminding you that my wife is off limits. Hurt her, Charlotte, and I will hurt you back. That is all."

She gave him a saucy wink. "Never fear, darling. I'd never jeopardize the success of my own ball just for petty revenge. But, tell me, does she really think you'll stay with her and play the attentive husband forever? How long does she think to keep you from my bed?"

"She's not keeping me from it, Charlotte. You are."

"You didn't say that last summer when I came to visit you."

It had been a drunken error in judgement. She'd cried pretty tears and told him how miserable and lonely she was. And he'd fallen for it like a gullible fool. Before she'd even gotten out of his bed, she'd asked him to deal with Lawrence Russell for her. He'd seen the writing on the wall then. She hadn't come to Boston Spa because she missed him. It had all been a ploy, and the last shred of feeling he'd had for her had faded into dust.

"That is a mistake that will not be repeated. Good day, Charlotte."

He mounted his horse, offered her a curt nod, and

then rode off. No doubt all of London would be talking about their confrontation, though it would likely be turned into an illicit tryst by the gossip mill. He hated London. Damn the vicar for running them from his home!

CHAPTER SIXTEEN

Althea was once again shopping with Sabine. It seemed to be an almost daily occurrence. Even if they did not make purchases, they still enjoyed the outing.

"You are very quiet," Sabine noted.

"Am I?" Althea asked. Of course, she knew that she was. Preoccupied by the missive she had received that morning, she could think of little else.

"What is pressing so heavily on your mind?"

"Lady Bruxton has decided to make us the guests of honor at her ball week after next," she admitted. "I received a note from her this morning, insisting that we must accept her invitation, as she had already told everyone that she was hosting in our honor. That if we fail to attend, it will only stir all that nasty gossip all over again."

The nasty gossip in question had been a rehashing in the society and gossip sheets about the nature of their marriage, about Sinclair's past betrothal to her, and others still speculating over Lord Bruxton's failing health and what Lady Bruxton's impending widowhood would mean for her. It was something she had no wish to consider. She certainly didn't want to spend an evening in the woman's ballroom, feted by false friends.

"That is a twisted business," Sabine agreed, shaking her head. "I cannot fathom what she means to gain from it."

"I've no notion. Those sorts of manipulations and machinations are beyond me. But I'm also certain that my husband is hiding something from me. He insists it's nothing to worry over and that I should treat it simply as a benevolent gesture, but I'm not entirely certain he believes that either. What strange hold does she have over him?"

Sabine shook her head sadly. "Mayville is a man inexorably tied to his past. There are painful secrets there that he has shared with no one, not even with Gray. I must wonder now if those secrets do not have something to do with her."

"Or, perhaps, believing her to be true, he confided them to her," Althea pondered. For some reason, the idea that he would confide such things to Lady Bruxton sparked her jealousy far more than the woman's beauty did.

As if sensing her upset, Sabine put down the ribbons she'd been eyeing. "Come along. Let's get an ice. I've an urge for something sweet, and I think you could use a treat."

They left the shop and made for Gunther's.

"Beyond Charlotte's scheming, how is everything else?"

Althea laughed. Sabine was not subtle. "You mean how are things specifically between Mayville and myself?"

Sabine grinned. "Well, I know that you have consummated your relationship. But what I do not know is if he's professed his love for you yet!"

"Most assuredly not! He desires me," she admitted. "I know that he does. But whether that is convenience because I am at hand or if it's a product of some deeper feeling is something I cannot hazard to guess. Nor will he admit it if that is the case. We both know that Mayville is content with our arrangement. Once I am with child, I shall happily remove myself from London to some destination as yet unknown, and we shall pursue our separate lives."

"He won't throw you out. I would never describe him as happy, but he has certainly been content of late. That alone speaks volumes," Sabine insisted. "And I do not think absence makes the heart grow fonder. I think familiarity does! The more you are with him the more he will come to depend on your nearness!"

"And the more I will come to depend on his," Althea replied. "I cannot afford to feel more for him than I already do, not when there is no assurance that those affections will ever be returned. I do not wish to hate him. I cannot think that the perpetual disappointment I would feel, loving him and never having his heart in return, would lead to anything but bitterness and hatred."

Sabine sighed heavily as they walked, her resignation with the thought of Althea's leaving a palpable thing. "You are the only real friend I have in London. Oh, I have the girls who work for me, but it's different since I married Gray. I'm no longer one of them, you know? And the other ladies of *the Ton* do not quite know what to make of me. I shall miss you terribly when you leave."

"Then, wherever I settle, you and Gray shall simply have to come visit. I would miss you both terribly as well. I have never known kinder people."

SHE'D KEPT to the shadows behind them as much as possible. No one ever noticed her. It was the thing that had allowed her to be of such service to Lady Bruxton for the longest time. In exchange for the information she gathered for her, she was permitted the luxury of existing within the inner circle of the one who ruled high society. Miss Penelope Dennings, wallflower, spinster and confidante of the most wanted and hated woman in all of high society.

But it had been more than worthwhile that day to blend into the background. She'd overheard the entire conversation between Lady Mayville and the Countess of Winburne—including the details of the bargain between Lord Mayville and his plain bride.

When the women reached Gunther's, such a crowded location where they would be pushed together in a way that would ensure her being recognized, Penelope made the choice not to follow them inside. Instead, she headed for Upper Brooke Street so that she might report all she'd heard to Charlotte.

Hailing a hack, once inside, she removed the drab, gray cloak that concealed her more fashionable clothing and the ugly bonnet that had hidden her hair. Her own bonnet, a very stylish one from the most sought-after milliner in all of London, had been left behind at Charlotte's that morning before she'd been given her task.

When the hack stopped in front of Charlotte's home, she was helped down by a footman, who had been watching for her arrival. She knew then just how eager Charlotte was for what she might have learned.

Climbing the steps to the house quickly, the butler opened the door and ushered her to the private drawing room that Charlotte used for her most intimate friends. It was a point of distinction to ever be invited into that room, and she had been there often. With what she'd learned that day, her position in the exalted circle of Lady Bruxton was secure.

The moment she entered, Charlotte, who had been pacing, halted and faced her. "Well?"

"He means to live separately from her but stay wed to her. They have an agreement that as soon as she is with child, she will depart London, and they will maintain separate households from that moment forward!" Penelope said hurriedly.

Charlotte's response was not at all what she'd anticipated. There was no giddy relief that the man was not in love with his wife. Instead, there was her furious temper.

A porcelain shepherdess went flying off a side table to crash against the fireplace surround. A vase of perfectly arranged roses crashed to the carpet, water soaking through to the parquet flooring below. Everything Charlotte came into contact with suffered her violent outburst until, at last, she sank to her knees on the floor and sobbed hysterically.

"He cannot stay married to her! I will not have it!"

"But, Charlotte, you cannot marry him. You have a husband," Penelope said. For her own part, she thought the rumors of Lord Bruxton's failing health were greatly exaggerated. The man was hale and hardy enough whenever she saw him. Those rumors, in fact, were spread by Charlotte herself. It was one of the ways that she ensured she would always be talked about and therefore always an object of curiosity.

"I don't want to marry him, you idiot!" Charlotte shrieked at her. "But he is supposed to want to marry me. He is always supposed to want me! And I could see it when I spoke to him in the park. He has fallen out of love with me. And a man only stops loving one woman when he has begun to care for another. He may not even realize it yet, but he is falling for her, and I cannot have that. I will not ever be thrown over that pale, insipid mouse!"

Penelope frowned at that. She had not found Lady Mayville to be pale and insipid. While she certainly was not the great beauty that Charlotte was, she had her own quiet loveliness. Not to mention the fact that she had been dressed very fashionably. Then again, she was being advised on her wardrobe by the Countess of Winburne, who had previously been the most sought-after modiste for all *the Ton*. Was it any wonder her clothing was perfection?

"It is impossible that he could stop loving you," Penelope offered, hoping to reassure her.

"I need to get them apart." Charlotte continued as if Sarah hadn't spoken at all. "And not an amicable parting. Sinclair is very sensitive to abandonment. No doubt that is the result of our broken engagement. If I can persuade her to leave him, he will never forgive her for it."

"But how would you do that?"

Charlotte smiled. "She loves him, doesn't she?"

Penelope nodded. "She thinks so. She expressed to the countess that she feared loving him while not being loved in return would make her hate him."

Charlotte nodded. Then, calmly, as if she hadn't just destroyed several very expensive items, she rose from the floor and brushed the wrinkles from her skirts. "Then, I have to make her believe that he will never love her. To do that, I shall only have to convince her that he still loves me. Is there anything else they said that might be useful? Do her friends and family call her anything special? A nickname or diminutive? It will add to the illusion of intimacy between Sinclair and myself."

"The countess called her Althea."

Charlotte's smile broadened into a very wicked grin, one that appeared almost diabolical. "Oh, that is perfect. When we spoke in the park, Sinclair called her Thea. And if everyone else calls her something different, it will be even more convincing! Sarah, you are an absolute angel to have done this for me! I cannot wait to see that little wretch running away from London with her tail between her legs. It's what she deserves for having the gall to take what it is mine!"

Penelope didn't feel like an angel. For the first time since agreeing to being Charlotte's eyes and ears, she felt very, very guilty.

CHAPTER SEVENTEEN

It was late evening when Sinclair returned home. She had thought it would be another dinner alone. There had been several of late. He would vanish to his club in the afternoons. It seemed the more physical intimacy they shared, the less intimacy they had of any other sort. He was determined to keep her at arm's length, and that told her all that she needed to know about his feelings for her.

"Ah," he said, entering the drawing room. "I had hoped to have a word with you before dinner."

"I am at your disposal," she said, hating how very true those words were.

"I've made some arrangements, Thea, for your future," he offered, crossing the room to the small cart laden with spirits. He poured himself a shockingly conservative measure of brandy.

"Oh? And what sort of arrangements are those?" she asked.

"Well, I've obtained a house in Bath. I thought—since

London society is not something you have any great interest in—that Bath, with its somewhat quieter society and slower pace, might be more to your liking. And there are numerous accounts now set up in your name so that, should anything happen to me, you will not be dependent upon me for your income."

"What might happen to you?"

"Well, one never knows, really. Regardless, these are things that I should have taken care of earlier, given our arrangement."

That dratted arrangement. "I see. Well, I shall certainly apprise you the moment I have news. We wouldn't want to drag this on any longer than necessary, would we?" She hadn't been able to keep the bitterness from her tone.

His expression hardened. "I am not a villain for granting you what you've asked for. Nor am I the villain for being a responsible husband and seeing to your future, in the event that something should happen to me! Or would you rather I ignore my responsibilities and leave you to the tender mercies of your father? How likely is he to welcome you back?"

Her eyes narrowed, and she bit out the words between clenched teeth. "Thank you very much for reminding me of all the many reasons why I did not wish to be married to you to start with! How foolish I've been to think these last few idyllic weeks were anything but a very temporary interlude! You can't be bothered to care about anyone else; that much is obvious."

"If I didn't care, I wouldn't have done this!" he snapped.

"This wasn't about caring for me! Don't pretend you did this because you cared! You did this because you're eager to be rid of me, and this will allow you to do so without guilt, because you will have discharged your duty!" she snapped back, her voice rising to a degree that she was fairly certain she had never reached before. He was utterly maddening.

The dinner gong sounded, halting whatever reply he'd intended to make. From the tightly clenched jaw to the anger blazing in his gaze, it was likely a blessed reprieve. Instead, he said, "I'm going in to enjoy my evening meal, after which I will go seek my own bed for the evening. Though, perhaps I ought to provide the stud service you require. The sooner I've managed to put a brat in your belly, the sooner we can stop shouting at one another."

The words cut her to the quick, because they were likely the most honest exchange that had passed between them in some time. Any faint hope she might have held that things could be different with them simply fled in that moment. Yet, despite that stinging pain, her newly discovered sense of pride would not allow her to be cowed by his harsh words or his flaring temper. She'd weathered worse, after all. Getting to her feet, she followed him into the dining room and took her place at the end of the table directly opposite him.

His only response was to arch one brow and observe

sardonically, "I see you are not in the mood to negotiate a truce."

"I wasn't aware we were at war," she answered, as the footman filled her wine glass. She could see by the servant's expression that they would all be eagerly dissecting the argument as the evening's entertainment. Sinclair was so used to his life as a privileged member of the peerage, he was simply oblivious to the people who kept his house running like a well-oiled machine.

"Funny, that's precisely what I thought we were doing when I walked into the house to find you tossing verbal volleys in my direction."

Althea shook her head. "If you'd been making arrangements for my future security because you cared about me, you might have included me in those arrangements or, at the very least, discussed them with me first. Instead, you arbitrarily decided where I am to live even when I do not live with you! Once again, Sinclair, you are high-handed, arrogant, and self-serving. What you did was not for my benefit. It—no, I—was simply an object to be marked off your agenda!"

He glowered at her but had no argument to refute her assertion. Whether he had intended it to appear that way or not, it was an accurate assessment. Then one of the footmen smothered a laugh behind a fake cough. Sinclair looked up, caught the rapt expressions on all of them as they looked on, and he snapped. "Get out, the lot of you. Get out now, and if I hear so much as a peep or a whisper, I'll sack the lot of you!"

"It isn't their fault we're behaving like children," Althea protested.

"And you will not say another word until we can do so privately," he hissed.

She laughed. "Now! *Now* you're concerned with respectability! A month ago, you were so stumbling-down drunk in an inn yard you couldn't tell the difference between a vicarage and a tavern!"

"A fact which you have benefited from greatly, have you not? You've certainly not complained about having someone else to scrub floors and do the washing!"

MAYVILLE KNEW, the very moment the words left his mouth, that they were a terrible mistake. Everything he'd said, from the moment he'd entered the house that night, had been a terrible mistake. She was right. He should have discussed her future with her, especially as he didn't really plan to be a part of it. Making assumptions about where she should live and how much she would require, those were decisions she was entitled to be privy to—not under the law, perhaps, but certainly under any sense of fairness.

As he watched, she pushed her chair back and rose. "I'm not very hungry, after all. I think I will retire for the night. Alone."

Before he could even consider what he was doing, he was out of his own chair and closing the distance between them. He caught her wrist before she reached the door and spun her about till she faced him.

"I have no wish to continue this conversation," she said.

"Then, do not," he said softly. And instead of uttering another word, which would surely come out wrong, he kissed her.

Hard and angry, that kiss had an edge to it that reflected everything they'd said to one another and everything that was left unsaid. But she didn't shy away from it. No, she kissed him back with the same ferocity. The animosity from only seconds earlier transformed in that instant to a raging passion.

By God, she drove him half mad. Challenging and often maddening, she could be, then sweet and tender or cold and indifferent. But she wasn't indifferent in that moment. It lit a fire in his blood.

Unable to think, unable to do anything but act on the basest of instincts, he simply pressed her back against the door and began tugging her skirts up. Her assistance with that task was all the confirmation he needed that she was just as eager. With the fabric of her gown bunched at her waist, he dropped to his knees before her and pressed his face against her mound, licking and gently biting at her plump lips. When she let out a broken whimper, and one of her hands grabbed at his hair, pulling it roughly, only then did he give her what she wanted—what she surely craved with the same hunger he did.

Parting the folds of her sex, he lapped at the hardened

bud until she was arching against him, calling his name. Heedless of anyone that might overhear, heedless of anything but the consuming need she felt, seeing her in such a state and knowing that he was responsible for it was the headiest of feelings. He wanted her to scream for him. He wanted her to be so wild with passion that nothing else mattered. And, so, he continued the onslaught, never giving quarter even when she begged. Even when she shattered, her release washing through her until her entire body was slack with it, he didn't stop. He drove her up and over that precipice again and again while she sobbed brokenly.

When his own need became too demanding, he rose, slid his hands beneath her thighs and lifted her. It was she who fumbled with the buttons of his breeches, until his shaft sprang free from the fabric, then he was driving into her even as he pressed her back against the door. With every thrust, the door banged loudly in the frame, and her cries echoed softly in the large dining room.

He kissed her again, his tongue invading the soft recesses of her mouth, claiming it as surely as he claimed her body. And then she was trembling against him, taken once more by the undeniable pleasure. He followed seconds later, his release leaving him shuddering as he pressed his body fully against hers to hold them both upright.

Only the sound of their ragged breathing filled the room as they both slowly returned to the present and to what had just passed between them. It had been consensual, but it had bordered on the knife edge of violent, a reflection of their complicated and, at times, contentious relationship.

"I'm sorry," he whispered.

"For this?" she asked, with a slightly bitter laugh. "This is the one thing we seem to get right. It's everything else that we get wrong."

"Not for this," he said, pressing his lips against her forehead in a gesture that was gentler than anything else that had passed between them. "For everything else, yes. But not for this."

She pushed against his chest, and he reluctantly stepped back from her, disentangling their bodies. He immediately regretted the loss of her warmth, the loss of that connection.

"I cannot do this with you," she said.

"You wanted this bargain between us, Thea. You asked for a child, and I am doing what is required to give you one," he replied flatly.

"I know that...but the cost might be too great. I didn't know what it would do to me. I didn't know that having this...intimacy with you would change me. But it has. I can't give you my body again and again without giving you the pieces of myself you do not want. You don't want my heart, Sinclair, nor do you want my soul, and now I have discovered that they are all far more connected than I had ever imagined."

He couldn't say anything. He certainly couldn't find the words to say what needed to be said. It was so much more than just physical. She was more than a way to slake his lust. But the words were locked inside him, dammed by years of pretending that he felt nothing but ennui and disdain.

She smoothed her skirts and then turned to exit the dining room, leaving him staring after her, with his heart in his throat and a world of regret pressing down on him.

CHAPTER EIGHTEEN

The Night of the Bruxton Ball

ALTHEA STARED at her reflection with complete disinterest. It didn't matter that her hair had been dressed more fashionably and more flatteringly than ever before. Nor did it matter that the dress Sabine had designed for her was true perfection. The rich plum color only reminded her of the dress Sinclair had procured for her after their night at the White Hart Inn. It reminded her of the moments when he could be kind.

Since that fateful night in the dining room, they had given one another a very wide berth. She would have her breakfast in her room, and he would have dinner at his club. The detente they had settled into over the past week had been cold and silent. How in heaven's name they would appear at this ball and pretend to be a happy newly wedded couple was beyond her.

"You look beautiful, my lady," Sarah offered and then, sympathetically, added, "But you do not look very happy."

"There is little enough to be happy about. I've no wish to go to this ball, Sarah. It's like willingly walking into a den of vipers. I cannot but think Lady Bruxton has something horrible planned," Althea admitted.

The maid tidied up the dressing table, putting away extra hair pins with more force than necessary. "I've heard about her. Her servants gossip something fierce, and they're always after gossip from this household. When cook sent some of the kitchen girls to the market, one of her maids was lying in wait for them, hoping to bribe something out of them. But they knew better. We all know better!"

"He shouldn't have threatened to sack the footmen that night," Althea sighed.

"Oh, no, it's not that, ma'am! He's got a temper, his lordship does, but this is a good house to work in, and he's a good employer to work for! We are well paid and get whole days off instead of half-days. None of the maids have ever had to run from him or his guests. He treats us like people and not like we were just pieces of the furniture."

It was all true. Despite his outburst of temper that night, a temper she had intentionally provoked, no less, she had observed how fairly treated the servants were. She'd also taken over the household accounts and knew that Sarah was speaking the truth. He paid them generously.

"Well, I am glad that you are all happy here and glad that he has your loyalty," Althea stated.

"Not just him, my lady. You have our loyalty too. I know things ain't quite right now, but you're good for his lordship. I believe that to my soul, I do. And I think, if you could both see your way clear of it, he would be good for you, too. You was so happy before. I know you can be again."

With that, the maid bustled out, and Althea was left alone with her own very bitter thoughts. She had been happy—as happy as she would permit herself to be. The truth of the matter was she didn't know how to just live in the moment and accept happiness as it came to her. She'd been so very busy preparing herself for looming disaster and heartache that, in many ways, she'd brought that disaster and heartache to fruition. Looking back at the argument that had so damaged things between them, she could accept that she'd played a very large role in bringing it about. He had been wrong to make such assumptions about her future, but if she were to be completely honest, the reason it had offended her so greatly had been that she was forced to face the fact that he was looking towards the end of their time together.

It had seemed a rejection to her in that moment, as if by planning for the outcome they had already agreed upon, he was somehow betraying her. And it was all because she no longer truly desired that outcome. Because, in the absence of his presence for nearly a week, when the distance between them seemed to be insurmountable, she could finally admit the truth: It was too late for her not to love him. Her heart already belonged to him, and she could only hope that it wasn't too late to repair the damage they'd done to their burgeoning relationship.

Determined to try, to at least attempt to repair that which was broken, she picked up the velvet, fur-lined wrap that had been created to match her gown and made her way downstairs. Her steps faltered when she reached the stairs. She could see him below, dressed in elegant evening clothes as he awaited her. He was beyond handsome, and her pulse skittered when she saw him, just as it always had whenever she'd chanced to see him walking through their small village. How much it had all changed since then, and how much it had all stayed the same!

He turned to face her, and she saw, for the barest hint of a moment, his gaze darken with hunger. Then his expression shuttered, and he wore the same sort of stolid response she had received from him during any chance meeting in the last week. Bracing herself for what would be a very long and difficult night, Althea descended the stairs and tried, with very little success, to harden her heart.

CONTRARY TO HIS OUTWARD EXPRESSION, he was anything but indifferent to her appearance. That fateful night at the White Hart, the first of their many remarkable clashes, he'd seen something in her that he hadn't anticipated—a fire that called to him. And, the following morning, when she'd emerged from the inn, wearing a dress that was remarkably similar to the one Sabine had fashioned for her for Charlotte's ball, that had been the first time he'd understood how desirable Thea truly was.

For so long, she'd hidden behind severe hairstyles and dowdy clothing, binding her breasts in that torture device of a corset so that she might appear as sexless as possible. Her father really should have been horsewhipped for doing those things to her, he thought. But he'd tormented her in his own way and likely deserved a horsewhipping of his own.

He'd been keeping his distance from her during the days and slipping into her bed at night, availing himself of all the warmth and passion she offered, while trying his damnedest to keep any sort of tender feelings at bay. She'd accused him of trying to discharge his responsibilities to her as a means of hurrying her exit from his life. Perhaps he hadn't done so consciously, but there was an undeniable truth to her assessment of the situation. But if the last week of terrible silence between them had taught him anything at all, it was that it was far too late for him to be shed of her without consequence. He missed her terribly, and she wasn't even gone from his home yet.

As she reached the bottom of the stairs, he took a deep breath and let it out slowly. "I have something for you," he said.

"You didn't need to," she protested.

"I did, in point of fact. You cannot go to a society ball without proper jewelry," he explained, moving to the small table where he'd placed the silk-lined box with the parure he'd commissioned for her. Simple and elegant, the confection of diamonds and pearls included a necklace, a tiara, a bracelet, and ear bobs. Opening the lid of the box, he presented it to her. "These should do nicely for you."

She blinked several times, taking in the matched jewels before looking up at him. "That is far too extravagant."

"It isn't, really," he said. "In comparison to many of the ladies present, this particular set will seem modest. But I knew that you would not want something as ostentatious as others might. I chose this set, Thea, as a gift for you. It is something lovely and something that I felt reflected the way I see you. Please accept it."

It was the humblest request he'd ever made in his life, and he waited with bated breath for her to reject it. But, after a long and seemingly immensurable pause, she reached out with one gloved hand and trailed her fingers over the diamond broach which connected the strands of pearls. "It's lovely."

Carefully, he withdrew the necklace and then placed the box in her hands. When she turned, presenting her back to him, he carefully positioned the necklace and then fastened the clasp for her. "It is where it belongs," he said. "I'll leave you to see to the rest of it. I would muss your hair, and that would be a truly unpardonable sin."

He stepped back and watched as she carefully donned the remainder of the pieces. Taking the box from her hand, he passed it to a footman. "We should go. No doubt there will be a line of carriages longer than Upper Brooke Street."

She nodded and draped her wrap about her shoulders. "I'm ready."

He wasn't. The longer he'd had to think about the coming event, the more he'd realized that Thea's initial misgivings were likely well founded. Charlotte, he'd come to understand, was a veritable cat. She might play the part of a delicate and simpering creature for men, whichever one struck her fancy or whichever one she needed something from in that moment, but when it came to other women—her competition—she could be vicious.

There was little doubt in his mind that it had nothing whatsoever to do with any tender feelings Charlotte might profess to have for him. Those were as false as she had ever been. He'd loved her when he was a boy, and as a man he could see her clearly for what she was.

Exiting the house, they moved quickly through the chilly evening air to the waiting carriage. Once inside the dim interior, they settled once more into a very uneasy silence. But she was the first to break it.

"I owe you an apology for my behavior," she said. "I was provoking and terribly rude to you when you had attempted to do what you felt was the right thing. I am sorry for that."

"You do not owe me an apology, Thea. I owe you one. I was taking the coward's way out and trying to simplify the process of your eventual departure. But the simple truth is that, when you leave, I shall miss you terribly. I know that without doubt now, as I have spent this past week missing you already."

"Then, ask me to stay," she whispered.

"I can't," he admitted, "because I sit here, even now, completely undeserving of you. But I will never ask you to leave. Isn't that enough?"

"I don't know," she answered, her voice raw with an honesty neither of them had intended.

"We do not have to decide anything now," he reminded her. "We will attend this farce of a ball. We will dance and be feted by people whom neither of us give a fig for. And, when we come home, I will spend the entire night showing you what it could be if you choose to stay."

CHAPTER NINETEEN

They were less than an hour into a ball that promised to drag on into the wee hours of the morning. While it was a ball in their honor, any married couple amongst *the Ton* was not expected to remain together at such an event. They were permitted to dance together for the opening set and would likely dance together for one more before the evening was out, but the rest of the time, they were all but sequestered from one another.

Thank heavens, Althea thought, that the Earl and Countess of Winburne were present. Had Sabine not been there to steady her nerves, she'd never have been able to endure it all. As if her thoughts had summoned him, Gray appeared, bearing two glasses of champagne, which he promptly handed to each of them.

"Mayville has been detained by Lord Ralston," he offered with a sympathetic grimace. "I'm sorry to inform you, Lady Mayville, of your impending widowhood, as your husband will likely be bored to death by the man!"

"Gray!" Sabine protested. "He's terribly nice. Dull, but still, so very nice."

"I've never met him," Althea confided, but she scanned the ballroom for a glimpse of Sinclair, hoping to see whom he was speaking with. She found them easily enough. Sinclair, taller than most men and with his elegant but indifferent posture, tended to stand out in the crowd. He was speaking with a very handsome young man who looked terribly earnest.

"What could they be talking about?"

"Rosedale Manor, most likely," Gray supplied, snagging another glass of champagne for himself from a passing footman.

"The family seat? What interest could he have in an entailed property?" Althea wondered.

"Rosedale isn't entailed," Gray explained. "It likely would have been, but the entail was broken with Mayville. His grandfather and father both died so close together there wasn't time to have the solicitor draw up the necessary paperwork to continue it. And I've no doubt whatsoever that Mayville will not do so. He'd be a happier man, I think, if he simply set a torch to it and walked away."

Althea let that sink in. The enormity of what Gray had told her was staggering. He did not have to live in a mouldering estate that he hated with every fiber of his being. Rosedale Manor was a self-inflicted punishment. He was tormenting himself for some dark family secret by remaining there.

"I had no idea," she admitted. "I just assumed that he

stayed there because he had no choice in the matter. He despises it so thoroughly, I could not imagine doing so willingly."

"He's a perverse creature at times," Gray said with a tight smile, clearly realizing that he had imparted problematic information. "Well, I shall leave you two and make for the card room. Perhaps I can rescue Mayville along the way."

When they were alone, Sabine said softly, "They stick together, don't they? But I suppose we do, as well. It doesn't change anything, really. He's not truly staying there by choice. Sometimes we make our own prisons, but they are prisons just the same."

"I certainly did with my father. He constructed it, with his abuse and tyranny, but I could have left. I could have taken my chances. I chose the security of the bus that I knew rather than the unknown that waited for me," Althea answered softly. "But I wish I could help him. Or, perhaps more correctly, I wish that he would learn to help himself. He should not bear the burden of others' guilt."

"None of us should, but we do just the same. Are things better between the two of you?"

Althea wasn't sure how to answer that. "I think we might have reached a new understanding tonight, but it is too soon to say for certain. He told me that he could not ask me to stay with him, but he did say that he would never ask me to leave. Why would he phrase it that way —'could not?'"

"Perhaps for the same reasons that he is punishing

himself," Sabine suggested gently. "A man who thinks himself unworthy will not ask to be loved. And when love is offered, he may very well turn away from it. But that doesn't mean it isn't needed just the same, or even reciprocated."

A bitter smile twisted her lips. "What a pair the two of us are. He thinks he is unworthy of being loved, and I was half mad for him before he even knew I existed."

"What?"

"I never told you. I never told anyone. But I would see him in the village, either when he was attending those wicked and scandalous prize fighting matches behind the butcher's shop or when he was simply out riding while I was paying calls for my father. And I was so infatuated with his golden perfection that I could not even speak when I saw him. I would never have dreamed that I would be here, that I would be his wife. But, some days, I think I am further from him now than I was in Boston Spa, before he knew my name."

Sabine leaned in close, "Wipe your tears, Althea. This is no place to shed them. They will only be used against you."

She hadn't even realized she was crying. Reaching up, she dashed them away quickly and turned away from her friend. She hadn't taken two steps before Sabine halted her.

"Where are you going? You cannot leave. As difficult as this is, we both know this ball was a strategic maneuver on Lady Bruxton's part. Everything you do is being monitored here!"

"I only need a moment. I'll be in the ladies' retiring room," Althea insisted. "I won't leave. I won't do anything desperate or foolish. No matter how much I may wish it."

With that, Sabine nodded and let her go. "I will find Mayville and Gray. It will be easier if we are all together, I think."

Althea only nodded as she turned away and made her way, as quickly as possible, through the throng of guests. To call the event a crush was a gross understatement. The entire ballroom was simply teeming with people.

When she'd finally managed to escape the crowd, she found herself in a wide corridor flanked with ornately carved doors. At the end of that hall, she could see a group of giggling ladies. The retiring room, naturally, would be beyond them. But before she could even step in that direction, a door opened, and Lady Bruxton appeared before her.

"Lady Mayville...Thea. I may call you Thea, I presume?"

Thea. There was only one person who used that shortened form of her name. When had Mayville spoken to Charlotte about her? "I would prefer Althea, actually."

"Oh! Of course. Thea is no doubt a diminutive only used by your most...intimate acquaintances," the hostess offered with a smile. "I thought we should have a word about your arrangement with Mayville and what will happen when it is complete."

A sick feeling rose in her stomach. "My arrangement?"

Lady Bruxton glanced over her shoulder at the giggling women, all of whom were watching them intently. "About your desire to have a child for him and then live separately after. Are you certain that is what you wish, my dear? Raising a child alone, a discarded wife, never free to move on and love again. I'm certain that a divorce could be obtained easily enough, given the strange circumstances under which your marriage occurred. Then you would be free to marry someone more of your own status. And, when I am widowed, Mayville and I would be free to show the world the true nature of our feelings for one another."

"You want me to pursue a divorce from my husband so that if—*if*—you are widowed, you may have him?" Althea asked incredulously.

She became aware of several things then. It was an ambush. The giggling women at the end of the corridor were no longer laughing. They were all watching the exchange between herself and Lady Bruxton with rapt attention. Lady Bruxton had arranged to have an audience for their confrontation.

"Well, he does love me, Althea. He has since we were so very young. And I daresay that, whether he remains wedded to your or not, he always shall. Just as I will always love him. I would have married him had my family not intervened and forced me to marry Bruxton. He's not a bad sort, but he's certainly not the husband that a wife can fall passionately in love with, is he? And Mayville...Sinclair, well, he's nothing if not passionate, is he? We had a very intimate exchange in

Hyde Park not long ago, in the trees just off Rotten Row."

"You're lying."

"How else would I have known about your arrangement, Althea?" Lady Bruxton reminded her gently. "He told me. He told me everything...and he's too honorable to ask you for this himself, though we both know it is what he would want."

It cut like a knife. She wasn't even certain it was true, but just thinking of it—that he might have left her bed and immediately engaged in a tryst with another woman —cut her to the quick.

"I am sorry, Lady Bruxton. I find that I am feeling unwell and will need to retire from your ball," Althea managed. "Good evening." Immediately, she turned on her heel and headed for the ballroom. She needed to get away, needed to flee before she said something truly horrid or humiliated herself in some other way. As if she could be more humiliated!

Althea didn't even stop to claim her wrap. Instead, she rushed past the stunned guests and made her way to the front doors. There, she pushed past servants and guests alike until she emerged into the cool night air.

"I need a carriage. A hack. Anything," she said to the footman standing there. "I must leave here at once."

"Take mine. I will walk. You are far too distressed to wait."

Althea turned to see the man her husband had been speaking with earlier, Lord Ralston. *He has very kind eyes*, she thought immediately. Soft and brown, framed by thick, dark lashes, they held a warmth and a gentleness that surprise her. "You do not know me."

"You are Lady Mayville, and your husband is an acquaintance," he said. "Clearly, you are distressed, and I can be of assistance. I shall inform him that I have lent you the use of my conveyance to see you home."

"No, please do not tell him. I will send word once I am safely home," she said. She needed a reprieve. If he knew she had left, he might come for her. Then again, he might not. And she honestly could not fathom which outcome would be worse.

He frowned at that. "It is no trouble—"

"We've had a...disagreement. I fear if he comes home immediately that disagreement will only continue. It is better this way, sir, that we both might have time to cool our tempers."

"Ah," he said, his expression shifting to one of sympathy and understanding. "Then, I wish you a peaceful evening, Lady Mayville, and all the time you require to soothe your nerves. Allow me to assist you?"

He helped her into the carriage that waited at the foot of the steps and then gave the driver instructions. "See Lady Mayville home, and then you are dismissed for the night, Charles. I shall walk home."

"Yes, my lord," the coachman replied.

"Number 114 Park Lane," Althea supplied. And then, within seconds, the coach was off, rolling slowly through the crowded streets of Mayfair, toward a house that she would never again call her home.

CHAPTER TWENTY

Mayville had left the ball and was headed back to Park Lane. He hadn't laid eyes on Althea in hours. He was worried, more so than he had anticipated. The evening had not gone at all as he'd envisioned, but Charlotte had made it a point to keep them separated. In retrospect, that was easy enough to see. What he didn't know was why. He'd made it perfectly clear to her that their relationship (if what had transpired between them could ever be called such) was firmly in the past. But Charlotte could be a perverse and contrary creature. Her selfishness was boundless.

Reaching his home, he disembarked from the carriage and climbed the steps, where he found the butler wringing his hands in the foyer. "What the devil is wrong with you?"

"Her ladyship has returned home and requested that several trunks be prepared for her use. Her maid is with her now so that they may begin packing."

He blinked at that. She was upset, certainly. That had been evident based on the hurried manner in which she had left the ball. Thank heavens that Ralston had broken her confidence and rushed to let him know. "Pardon?"

"Packing, my lord," the butler repeated. "She has expressed that she intends to depart London tomorrow morning."

"The devil she will," he snapped, and moved toward the stairs, taking them two at a time. When he reached her chamber, the noise level within was a testament to the flurry of activity. As he stood there in the hallway, a footman rushed past him, carrying a trunk. "Drop that at once!"

The footman glanced up, startled, and placed the trunk on the floor with a heavy thump. "Yes, my lord. Is aught amiss?"

"A great deal is amiss, it would seem. Leave, and take them all with you," he said, making a sweeping gesture toward the bevy of servants scurrying about. Then he strode into Thea's room without knocking. Two maids were there. They instantly stopped what they were doing and looked up at him in terror. "Get out."

"Stay," Thea countered.

"This is not a conversation I mean to have in front of the maids. You will leave this room or seek new employment," he snapped. "I am still master of this house, regardless of what you may have heard."

The maids immediately put down the garments they

had been folding and left the room. Thea glared at him, her anger a palpable thing.

"Once a bully, always a bully," she spat. "You're more of a hypocrite than even my father."

"That requires explanation. How am I hypocrite, Thea?"

"How are you not? You spoke of how wrong it had been of you to make decisions about my future without consulting me, but you've never stopped making them, have you? You and Lady Bruxton!"

"What the devil does that mean?"

"You were with her in Hyde Park," she said. "I know all about your clandestine meeting with her!"

"Yes, I met with her in Hyde Park. That doesn't explain why you are so unreasonable—"

"How did she know, Sinclair?"

"Know what?" he demanded, tired of the word games. It was like being an actor in a play, without the benefit of a script.

"How did she know about our arrangement?"

It was like a punch in the gut. "I don't know, of course. You can't think I would tell her!"

"I can't think how else she would know. But I'm tired. I'm tired of pretending that we can make this something it isn't. We are not meant to be together. There is no world in which our being married to one another makes any sort of sense at all! So, if you want a divorce or an annulment, I won't try to stand in your way."

"I don't want a divorce or an annulment! For heaven's sake, Thea, you could be carrying my child even as we speak. How can you think, after what we've shared, that I would grant such a thing?" He felt like everything was spinning out of control, and he didn't even know how or why. None of it made any sense.

"The house in Bath," she said. "Is it ready for occupancy?"

"Do not do this, Thea. Please. Be reasonable."

"Is it available for immediate occupancy?" she demanded again.

She would not budge, he realized. Whatever had transpired that night, her decision was made. Stubborn, intractable, and more obstinate than a team of mules, there would be no swaying her. "Yes. It's ready. The lease is signed, it's fully furnished, and you may take servants with you from here—those who wish to go. I'll replace them through an agency once you've gone."

"Tomorrow morning. I want to leave as soon as possible. I don't wish to be a bother or be in your way."

A bitter laugh escaped him. "I am bothered, Thea. Rest assured, I am bothered. And I doubt that I shall ever be anything less. As for being in someone's way, consider this house yours for the night. I will sleep elsewhere and return tomorrow after you have departed. I see no point in goodbyes."

"Of course you don't," she snapped. "I'll leave the jewelry."

"You bloody well will not. It was a gift."

"I don't want it!"

"Then throw it in the damned Thames!" he shouted as he stormed toward the door. He slammed it behind him with such force that the wooden frame cracked. It didn't even slow his steps as he headed for the stairs.

"My lord?" The butler asked, approaching him with yet more worried handwringing.

"Lady Mayville will need a retinue of servants to attend her in Bath. Assemble them from the household here, if enough are willing to make the move, then hire replacements as you see fit."

"You have chosen all the servants in this household, my lord—"

"I will not be here. I'm returning to Boston Spa, departing immediately, and will likely not be back in London for some time."

The butler paled. "Yes, my lord. I'll see to it. Godspeed on your journey, sir. Is her ladyship well?"

"She is the devil. I'm certain that makes her well enough," he snapped and then turned to make his way through the kitchens, to the stables beyond. He would saddle his own mount and ride through the night, but he would not spend another moment in London, the site of all his present misery.

CHAPTER TWENTY-ONE

They had reached Bath after three long and miserable days in the carriage. The rain had slowed their progress terribly on the first day, and on the second day, Althea had been so ill that she could barely move from the bed. Now, reaching the city, with its picturesque hillside views and endless array of classically inspired structures in the soft shades of creamy Bath stone, she wished she could be more excited about the change of scenery.

"It's lovely, isn't it?"

"Yes, my lady," Sarah said.

The house was in the Royal Crescent. A note had been delivered from Sinclair's solicitor the morning before she left, along with letters of credit and a significant amount of coin for the journey. Given how they'd parted, his thoughtfulness in seeing to her comfort on the journey was something of a shock. But, then, he had what he wanted, she supposed, at least ultimately.

Recalling how upset he'd appeared, she could only

assume it was a matter of inconvenience. He was a man with lusty appetites, after all, and having a willing wife at his disposal, given that his lover had a husband to whom she was bound, would likely have made life simpler for him. She'd been unwittingly fulfilling the role of mistress for him, offering a place that he might slake his lusts when the woman he truly desired was unavailable.

Just thinking it, those hateful words turning over and over in her mind, hurt so terribly that it robbed her of breath. She let out a soft gasp as she wrapped her arms about herself.

"Is it the babe?"

Sarah's strange question penetrated the haze her mind. "Babe?"

"My lady, you were ill all day yesterday and most of this morning. You've not had your courses since you come to London, which was more than a month back. Unless you had them right before you come to London... Well, what else could it be?"

She swayed, not because of the coach's movement, but because what the girl had said to her rocked her so deeply. The thought had not occurred to her. She'd been so lost in the passion, and then in the terrible betrayal, counting the days had been the furthest thing from her mind.

"Oh, dear lord. Oh, dear, sweet lord," she murmured.

"Oh, I though you knew!" Sarah cried in alarm.

"I hadn't thought. I hadn't even dreamed."

"His lordship will be very happy, I think," the maid offered. "Perhaps this will help to bridge the gap—"

"I don't want him to know. Not yet. If he knows, he will come here, and I cannot face him, Sarah. Not now. I don't have the strength," she admitted brokenly.

"What did he do, ma'am? I can't think what might have been so awful!"

"He loves another," she admitted. "He loves another, and through my own foolishness, I love him."

"I don't think that's true. I can't believe it. He's so very different with you, ma'am."

"Is he? Because he confided in her, Sarah, about things that should have been personal and private between us. I can't forgive him for leaving my bed and going to her. But, more than that, I can't forgive him for sharing with her the details of our personal agreements. What purpose could he have had for doing so, other than to reassure her of his affections for her? Or to aid her in humiliating me?"

"Perhaps there's another explanation."

"I can't think of one. I wish I could. If I could, I might have hope," she admitted.

"I'll keep your secret, my lady. But secrets such as that can only be kept for so long."

"I'll deal with that when the time comes."

The maid nodded, and they lapsed into silence.

The enormity of it, the very idea that she might have his child growing inside her, was only beginning to sink in. It was a double-edged sword. While having a connection to him that could never be broken was a balm to her shattered heart, his absence in their lives would be a daily reminder of his betrayal, and that pricked at her pride and renewed her anger again. She could feel the bitter-ness welling inside her.

"I must find a way to forgive him," she whispered. "I cannot hate him forever. I cannot let my anger fester as it is now. It will devour me alive."

———

IT HAD TAKEN him three days to reach Boston Spa. Three days to think about what had transpired, to replay it again and again in his mind. Those three days had also given his temper time to settle, but that was doing nothing to ease the hurt. She had hurt him. It was some-thing no one had managed to do in a very, very long while. The last person to do so, in fact, had been Char-lotte. Her rejection of him immediately following his father's passing, though heaven knew it had been for the best, had hurt him, despite his relief at not having to be the one to reject her.

He'd thought then, mistakenly, that it would restore her if he were to break their engagement. But as the years had progressed, he'd watched her flit from one affair to the next, always coming back to him when she needed help with her scandal-courting family after her husband had washed his hands of them. That was when he'd seen the truth of Charlotte. She loved no one but herself, and the great love affair he'd built for them in his mind had been naught but a fairytale.

And he'd never dreamed to feel anything for Thea, save for relief at her absence. At their first true meeting, when he'd finally managed to crawl out of his cups, he had expected her to be a teetotaling harridan who would make his life hell. Instead, she'd been sweet, naive, funny, endearing, passionate... Still a harridan, at times, but one with whom he could have easily coexisted in what he could only describe as happiness. In truth, happiness was something he barely had a passing acquaintance with. Yet, in one fateful evening tainted by Charlotte's presence, all that had vanished.

It didn't take a great deal of intelligence to realize that he had greatly underestimated his former lover. Charlotte didn't want him, but she didn't want anyone else to have him. *Like a spoiled child with a discarded toy*, he thought bitterly. He would own that his gullibility regarding her blackened nature was a contributing factor. But a greater contributing factor, to his mind, was that Thea hadn't trusted him. She had taken whatever Charlotte might have said to her at face value and never considered that there might be another alternative. She'd displayed, with remarkable aplomb, just how little faith she had in him.

There was a quieter voice in his mind, one that he did not wish to listen to, that reminded him how very little reason he'd given her, or anyone else, to have faith in him. But he was indulging in self-pity, and that sort of brutal honesty about his own failings did not allow him to wallow with the sort of enthusiasm he preferred.

Dismounting in front of Rosedale, he looked at the chipped mortar and clogged gutters. The house wasn't falling apart fast enough to suit him. And in his current state, a bit of destruction would be a welcome reprieve.

Bending forward, he retrieved a large stone from the graveled drive and hurled it with both force and accuracy. It crashed against the window of the morning room, a room he rarely had reason to occupy. The glass shattered, and the wind billowed the sheer curtain inside. Strangely satisfying, he picked up another stone and repeated the gesture.

By the time he'd shattered every pain of glass in that window, the servants were standing on the porch, watching him with a strange mixture of curiosity and fear. No one knew what to make of him in that moment, and no doubt, they were all wondering what had become of their erstwhile mistress.

"Lady Mayville has elected to retire to Bath for the remainder of...well, forever," he offered with a grim facsimile of a smile. "I'll be in my study. Bring me brandy."

"A glass, my lord?"

"A barrel."

CHAPTER TWENTY-TWO

Four Months Later

CHARLOTTE WAS PACING the floor again. In her hands, she held the shredded remnants of a letter. "Why won't he read them?"

"Perhaps he had deeper feelings for Lady Mayville than you realized?"

The suggestion had come from Mary, Lady Peckham. It was greeted with a rage unlike anything Penelope had ever witnessed. Charlotte's temper, always volatile, had been positively incendiary since Lord Mayville had fled London. In response to Lady Peckham's gently voiced question, Charlotte began hurling things directly at the poor woman. She ripped the pillows from the settee and began shredding them, feathers flying everywhere in the small room.

"He can't love her! He promised to love me forever!"

she shouted. "No man has ever rejected me! No man! And Sinclair Wortham will not be the first!"

Penelope felt the guilt welling up inside her again. Might they have been happy if she hadn't interfered on Charlotte's behalf? Without her spying and carrying tales, would Lord and Lady Mayville still be residing together, happily married? It was a question without answer. She had interfered, and what-ifs were an impossible game.

"Forgive me, ladies. I've developed a terrible megrim. I must go," Penelope said, rising from the needlepoint-covered chair that was her normal spot for their morning gathering.

"You cannot leave me, Penelope!" Charlotte hissed accusingly. "I need you here! You are my right hand, after all."

"I cannot be that today, Charlotte. Forgive me," Penelope said, and made for the door. She didn't expect that it would go well, but she was not prepared for the ultimatum that followed.

"If you walk out on me now, Penelope, in my hour of need, you will never be permitted to return," Charlotte said haughtily. "No true friend would desert me so!"

"You have no true friends," Penelope said bluntly. "You have people that you have bullied and manipulated into toadying for you. And I am done with it. I have a headache, and I mean to leave. If you are such a terrible friend, Charlotte, that you do not even care when someone who has been by your side for months is ill, then I want no part of your friendship. Good day, ladies."

Penelope stepped through the doors of that morning room and into the center hallway of Bruxton House. She was both terrified and relieved. She'd done it. She'd freed herself from Charlotte, but at what cost?

You are freed from Charlotte, but you have amends to make yet.

That little voice in her mind was all the urging she needed. Rushing from Bruxton House, she stepped outside into the morning air and immediately made her way toward the home of the Earl of Winburn. It was early yet to call, but it wasn't really a social visit, she reasoned. It was a confession.

THE EARL OF WINBURN was having his breakfast and reading his correspondence as the Countess of Winburn was reading hers. They did not sit at opposite ends of the table, but rather sat side by side in the small breakfast room. His letter was from Mayville. Hers was from Althea. Wordlessly, as each of them reached the end of their respective letters, they traded them. There was a great deal of head shaking and tongue clucking.

"They've certainly made a muddle of it," Gray observed.

"He's made a muddle of it. He and that viper, Lady Bruxton!" Sabine shot back. "Poor Althea. She's miserably heartbroken."

"He fares no better. Both are too stubborn to ever see reason." Gray reached for his teacup and lifted it to his lips. Before taking a sip, he added, "Not that you'd know anything about stubbornness. Why, you've no more than a passing acquaintance with that flaw."

She didn't take the bait. Instead, Sabine smiled at him. "Should you like to test how stubborn I can be about opening my bedchamber door for you?"

"Our bedchamber," he corrected and leaned over to kiss her cheek. "We both know you'd never lock me out of it."

He was right, drat him. "Fine, I admit it. I would not. But you are stubborn as well."

"Of course I am. I would never dream of denying it. The question now, my dear, is what do we do to fix this? They are our dearest friends, and they are terribly unhappy."

"What can we do?" he asked. "They are entitled to make their own choices, however foolish we might think them."

It was a conversation they'd had many times over in the past months. But based on the contents of Sarah's last several letters, simply waiting on them to come to their senses was no longer an option. "And if it only impacted them, I would agree, but…"

It was a terrible breech of confidence to relay what she was about to. In fact, Althea herself had never shared the news. She'd received a very troublesome note only two days earlier from her friend's maid, confessing her mistress's secret. Althea was with child, and she was faring poorly. Sick at all hours of the day and night, she could hardly rise from her bed on most days.

"I'm not supposed to know. Althea has told no one. I only know because Sarah, her maid, wrote to me out of fear for her mistress."

"And what is it that you are not supposed to know, Sabine?" he asked suspiciously. "Has she betrayed him?"

"Oh! You're infuriating. Of course she hasn't! She's in love with him!"

"And he's in love with her and pickling himself in enough brandy to float an armada," Gray protested. "Love doesn't prevent them from being stupid."

He was absolutely correct, of course.

"She's with child," Sabine stated simply. "And her health is suffering greatly from it. I fear that her unhappiness is contributing to that. And, more than that, I fear what will become of Mayville if something happens to her before they make amends."

Her husband was silent for a moment, then he sighed with resignation. "What would you have me do? I know you've formulated some sort of plan."

Sabine looked back at Mayville's drunken, rambling letter. "Well, you will need to go to Boston Spa and get him sorted out first. He's too drunk now to see reason."

"And what will you do?" he asked gently.

"I shall be taking the waters in Bath, it seems. The season is almost over, after all. No one will think twice of us leaving a bit early."

At that moment, the normally unflappable butler entered the breakfast room and appeared to be...well, flapped. "Is there a problem?" Sabine asked.

"There is a young woman here to see you, my lady.

She insists it is an urgent matter and that it relates to the very serious situation with Lord and Lady Mayville."

"Is it Lady Bruxton?" Sabine demanded, eager to give the troublemaking woman a piece of her mind.

"No, madam. It is a Miss Dennings," the butler replied.

"Show her to the morning room, and I shall be along shortly."

Gray was frowning. "The only Miss Dennings that I am aware of is a bosom companion to Lady Bruxton. This does not bode well."

"Agreed," Sabine concurred as she rose from her chair. "And that is why I should see to her immediately and discover what I can about Lady Bruxton's plan."

Gray shook his head. "This girl cannot be trusted."

"Oh, I'm well aware. I'm also aware, as you may not be, that Lady Bruxton has a revolving door of bosom companions. Most never last more than six months. She drives them away with her demand for attention and her temper."

"How do you know that?"

She grinned. "Dressmakers are barely above servants, my dear, at least in the eyes of some. I've seen sides of Lady Bruxton most in society would never dream of—and I do not mean her figure."

Sabine left the breakfast room, her husband chuckling behind her, and made her way to the morning room, where Miss Dennings awaited her. When she opened the door, she saw the very teary-eyed young woman pacing worriedly. Immediately, Miss Dennings looked up and halted her steps so abruptly she nearly stumbled.

"I've done a terrible thing," she confessed.

Sabine smiled softly. "We've all done terrible things, my dear Miss Dennings. The question is what can you do to make it better? Sit, and we can discuss it reasonably."

Half an hour later, after copious amounts of tea and many wasted minutes comforting the distraught young woman, Sabine had the whole of it.

"And that is why I came here today," Miss Dennings said, her breath still hiccupping from her many, many tears. "I felt so terrible about what I had done. I truly thought she loved him and that he'd played her false by promising to wait for her until she was widowed."

Sabine sighed heavily. "Miss Dennings, Lady Bruxton has been bemoaning her impending widowhood since her wedding breakfast. All the scandal sheets talk about how frail Lord Bruxton is, yet when you see him, he is dancing a jig and speaking with great enthusiasm about when he can next get to the countryside for a spot of hunting. Lady Bruxton wants to be a widow, I think, but wishing for something does not make it true. And her wish for Lord Mayville to be madly in love with her and pining for her because she chose to marry another...well, that hasn't been true either."

"Does he love Lady Mayville? Have I played a part in separating a couple that would otherwise have been happy?"

"They have a complicated relationship," Sabine admitted. "They have very deep feelings for one another, but right now, all of that is terribly muddied through their own stubborn pride, as well as the interference of others. But I will go to see Lady Mayville and, best as I can, explain the situation to her. I cannot do that and keep your involvement a secret from her. You do understand that."

"I do," Miss Dennings replied tearfully. "Please convey my deepest apologies to her. I thought... Well, I only wanted to be liked. And if I did what Charlotte asked, she would like me. But I've come to realize that she doesn't like anyone. Perhaps not even herself. And I'd rather have a clear conscience than popularity."

Sabine smiled at her, a true smile filled with warmth. "That is a credit to you, Miss Dennings. It is easy to be swept away when a person is charming and beautiful, whether that person is a friend or a potential suitor. Appearances often hold more sway than their character."

Miss Dennings wiped the last of her tears away. "What an unfortunate truth that is, Lady Winburne. And of course you must tell Lady Mayville of my involvement. Anything that can help set it all to rights! She will hate me, but it is no less than I deserve."

Sabine rose to her feet as Miss Dennings did and walked the young woman to the door. "You are not hated. You were misguided, and no doubt, in time, all of that can be forgiven. Be kinder to yourself, Miss Dennings. We all fall short from time to time."

CHAPTER TWENTY-THREE

Rosedale Manor, Boston Spa

MAYVILLE RESTED his aching head upon the cool floor. All the curtains were drawn, and the room was almost entirely black, save for the single crack of light penetrating those drapes like a blazing inferno to his bleary eyes.

Placing his hands under him, he pushed his body up from the floor. As he did so, his feet sent an empty bottle skittering over the bare floor. He was in an unused part of the house, so the carpets were all rolled up, and the wood floor was freezing under his bare feet. Everything was covered with dust. Well, not everything. The shattered remains of various pieces of furniture littered the room, along with destroyed sections of plaster. Behind the plaster was the dark, rough-hewn wood of the original Tudor structure that had predated the baroque grandeur that his grandfather had felt reflected their status.

Thoughts of his antecedents made his stomach roil, and he dropped his head once more to the floor. He hadn't been sober in days. While the entire four-month separation from Thea hadn't seen him deeply in his cups on every single day, the past week had been the worst. *Since the bloody letter had arrived.*

Recalling the icy tone and his wife's cool words made him livid all over again. She'd simply reminded him that she was amenable to either a divorce or an annulment but that she wished for him to keep her apprised of his choice so that she might understand what would be expected of her. He wanted to throttle her. He wasn't divorcing her. He damned well wouldn't be seeking an annulment, either, given that he'd have to deny bedding her. That was a fact he'd never willingly deny, and he wasn't about to let her do so either.

He took two steps, and his stomach turned over. To keep from falling down, he had to grab onto the splintered bed post. It shifted, and he landed on the floor, flat on his arse. And that is where he sat, cursing her, cursing himself, and cursing the copious amount of brandy he'd consumed, when Gray walked in.

"You're a damned wreck," he observed flatly.

"Were you invited?" Mayville asked sharply. Too sharply. He placed one hand to his head to see if it had actually split open.

"I have an open invitation. Or did you rescind it when you elected to be an idiot?"

Mayville lay back down, lowering his head gingerly to the floor. "Leave me to die quietly, please."

"You're not dying. Not today. Not for some time to come, I should think. You're going to get up, sober up, take a bath because you reek, and then we're going to Bath so you can beg your wife's forgiveness."

That got him up off the floor. Headache and rolling stomach aside, he would not tolerate that insult. "I'll go to hell first!"

"How is that any different?" Gray demanded, sweeping his hand about the room. "You're living in a house that, apparently, time was not depreciating quickly enough, so you've lent it a helping hand! You drink yourself into misery by night, suffer through the day, and start all over again. You have made your own hell, Mayville, and I am here to drag you from it, whether you like it or not. Men facing impending fatherhood are required to at least pretend responsibility for a bit!"

"Now, listen here," Mayville insisted. "I am a man fully grown, and I can decide how to live my own life. If I want to drink morning, noon, and night, it is my right to do so! And no one, not you, not Thea—Wait. What did you say?"

"Coffee, bath, and then we talk," Gray said. "Actually, bath first. You really do reek to the heavens."

Mayville said nothing. What could he say? It was likely true. In fact, he was fairly certain it was true. No one could consume that much brandy and not smell. Climbing to his feet, he followed Gray from the room and then looked about. He was in the east wing of the house, a place he hadn't been in years. "How the devil did I even wind up here?"

"No one knows, but the servants heard you destroying the furnishings sometime after midnight. Several of them left. Two thought you'd gone mad and would murder them in their beds, and another thought it wasn't you at all but that the house was inhabited by ghosts," Gray explained. "Your butler is perturbed, incidentally."

He didn't care. Not in the slightest. "How did you know? Did she tell you?"

Gray turned back to face him, and his pity was easy enough to read in his expression. "No, she did not, nor did she tell Sabine. Her maid, who does know and is ostensibly keeping her secret, wrote to Sabine and confessed the whole of it. Not to gloss over it all, but apparently it is not going well for her. She is quite ill. What that means, I cannot say. But I think it behooves to move a bit faster and leave for Bath as soon as possible."

"She won't see me," Mayville said. "And if she's ill, what if seeing me only makes her worse?"

"I do not think that it will, not if you're in a frame of mind to be humble once we get there. It won't kill you to eat a bit of crow. If that brandy you've swilled hasn't killed you, nothing will. Once I can stand to smell you, I'll you everything else I know."

"It can wait until we're on the road. Get everything ready for us to depart. If what you say is true, the sooner we leave, the better."

ALTHEA WAS IN HER BED, staring up at the ceiling once more and praying that she would not vomit again. Why anyone thought to call this morning sickness was a mystery to her. It was morning sickness, noon sickness, afternoon, evening and night sickness. There was not an hour of the day, it seemed, that she was not on her knees, retching into a chamber pot.

A knock sounded at the door, and she called out weakly for the person to enter. Her assumption, that it would be Sarah, could not have been more wrong. Sabine entered, looking elegant and lovely as always. Instantly, Althea felt worse. Just looking at her friend in her fashionable traveling dress and perfectly coiffed hair made her terribly aware of her own appearance. Lank hair in braids, her night rail disheveled and her face paler than the linens she currently rested upon, she would look like she was at death's door.

"What are you doing here?" she asked. "You should not have come. I am very ill, and I would hate to pass that illness to you."

"You are incapable of passing along what you have caught, my dear," Sabine replied flatly. "I know what ails you, Althea, and do not think to deny it."

"Sarah," Althea said.

"Indeed, Sarah. But I would have come regardless of her letter, and I would have easily guessed what is the matter with you. No one can be that ill and have a belly that round. You cannot hide it forever, you know. The truth will always come out. And it is truth which has brought me. Mayville did not betray you to Charlotte. Lady Bruxton had set her spies on us, it seems."

She was too tired, too weak, and her brain too fogged from lack of any decent sleep for weeks at a time. "What are you talking about?"

"Miss Penelope Dennings. She was one of Charlotte's squadron of debutantes—all carefully chosen to show her in her most advantageous light. She never picks the prettiest girls, only those who can be easily eclipsed by her but with nice enough features that they are forgettable and draw no notice."

She recalled the bevy of young women at the end of the corridor the night she'd been confronted by Lady Bruxton. "One of them spied on us?"

"We were perhaps not as discreet in our discussions of your circumstances as we ought to have been. I can recall several occasions where we talked of your arrangement in vague terms in dress shops or other public places," Sabine explained, stepping deeper into the room until she could sit on the edge of the bed. "If a person followed us for long enough and listened hard enough, the details would not have been difficult to put together."

"Then how did she know that he called me Thea? He is the only one to do so," Althea insisted. She did not want to have hope. Not now, when they were so very far apart and the chasm between them too great to bridge.

"When he arrives, you may ask him."

Althea shook her head violently and immediately regretted the choice. A wave of nausea assailed her that had her once more leaning from the bed to heave into the chamber pot. But the contents of her stomach were long since gone.

Sabine moved to the washstand and returned with a cold cloth, which she pressed to her forehead. "Have you called for a physician? Surely you cannot go on this way."

"I've called for two different physicians, and both simply shrugged as if this is just a normal part of carrying a child and I was being hysterical," Althea said bitterly. "And I have, daily, wished this misery on them both."

"Then, we shall not get another physician. We will instead get a midwife, someone who will be more sympathetic to your plight. Rest, Althea, and I will see to it. You will need your strength in the coming days, I think. I should expect them here by the end of the week."

"I don't want to see him. Perhaps he didn't betray me to her, but in the end, he still wants to be with her, and if he knows that I am carrying his child... I don't want him that way. If I'll only have him out of obligation, I'd rather not have him at all."

"You are both impossibly foolish," Sabine said firmly. "You squander love. You love him, and I believe, in my heart of hearts, he loves you. But you are both so unwilling to risk your pride, you will not admit your feelings—not to yourselves or one another. And now there is a child to think of. A child needs both parents to love it and treasure it. If Gray and I should ever be so lucky..."

Althea watched as Sabine sank back down onto the bed once more, tears in her eyes. "What is it?"

"Before Gray and I married, I had been carrying his

child. I lost it not long after, a fact that I grieve constantly. All I want is to have that with him, to have a family and see his eyes light up when he looks at our child. You can have that, Althea. You can have that happiness if you will simply be brave enough to reach for it!"

"I'm sorry for what you have lost, for what you are suffering. But Mayville is not Gray. Gray is a good man, an honorable one!"

"And so is Mayville, only he does not know it. He punishes himself for the sins of others and believes that he is tainted by their misdeeds. It is illogical, but then, you are a lovely woman, and yet every time your father called you plain or ugly, you believed him. We are all illogical when it comes to our families," Sabine argued.

Althea had no answer for that. It was all completely true and more damning for it. "I will think about it. That is all I can promise."

Sabine nodded. "Then, I shall go see to securing a midwife for you—one who will actually help you."

Althea watched her go, and while her own misery pressed heavily on her, the tears she shed in that moment were for her friend. She felt ungrateful for complaining of her sickness when that sickness was the result of having the thing she had always wanted and the very thing Sabine would gladly suffer any discomfort for. And then she did something she had not done since she'd left her father's house: She said a prayer. She offered it up for her friend, that one day she might have the promise of a child of her own.

CHAPTER TWENTY-FOUR

It took longer than expected to reach Bath. By the time they finally arrived, they'd been on the road together for more than a week. Mayville was at a point where he wasn't even certain he could accurately call Gray a friend anymore, so sick he was of his company.

When they reached the house at the Royal Crescent, Gray didn't even stop. He simply kept on riding toward his own home nearby, with a cocky salute.

"Damn him," Mayville muttered as he dismounted. When his feet hit the paving stones, he simply stood there for a moment, willing the blood to rush back to his extremities. He loved riding and always had. But more than a week in the saddle had left him regretting the decision not to travel at least partly by coach. Abominable weather had slowed them, countless storms making the roads muddy and treacherous.

A moment later, the door opened, and the butler stepped out. He was instantly recognizable, of course, as he'd previously been the first footman at the house in London. Apparently absconding with a runaway wife was an efficient route to promotion through the ranks.

"My lord," he said in greeting, as a footman rushed past him to take the reins.

"James?"

"Jones, sir. Jones."

"Right. Jones. How long have you worked for me?"

"Seven years, my lord," he replied.

"I see," Mayville said. "Well, seven years is a long enough time for me to disclose something personal to you. I can't walk up those steps. Not now. Give me about ten minutes to get my legs under me before you announce anything, would you?"

The butler blinked. "Oh. I take it you've had a very long and arduous journey, sir."

"Indeed. Indeed. I'm just going to mill about here in the street for a bit."

"Certainly, my lord. A chamber has been readied for you, and I shall immediately have a hot bath drawn. No doubt you will want to be less muddy and less...horse scented when you see her ladyship. She is very sensitive to smells at this point in time."

Mayville blinked. Had one of his own servants just told him that he smelled? Shaking his head, he simply walked across the street to the parkland opposite it. He moved gingerly, his muscles protesting the days of being cramped in the same position. Though, if he were honest, he would admit it wasn't simply the journey.

His four-month-long bout of self-pity had seen him

rarely leaving his house. He hadn't attended the fights, ridden his horse, or even seen daylight on most days. He'd holed up in his house with brandy and his own miserable thoughts while nursing his fury at her. At least now he partially understood her reasoning, though it still rankled that she'd had so little trust in him.

When at last he didn't feel like his knees would buckle and that he might actually make it up the steps under his own steam, he turned and headed back towards the house. A movement on one of the upper floors caught his eye, and he looked up. She stood at the window, her face a pale shadow behind the glass. But once she'd been caught, she dropped the curtain and stepped back, hidden once more.

Mayville sighed heavily. He'd missed her face. Missed the sound of her voice. He'd missed touching her, kissing her, talking to her. He'd just missed her, dammit. And he couldn't live the way he had for the past four months. After Gray had pulled him out of his drunken stupor a week earlier, he'd had more consecutive days of not being falling-down drunk than he'd had in the entire time since he'd left London. It wasn't a state he could return to. That was no way for a man to live. And it was certainly no way for a father to behave. Whatever agreements they'd made in the past were forgotten. New agreements would be forged, and they wouldn't involve the foolishness of separate lives. Without her, he had no life.

ALTHEA HAD BEEN WATCHING HIM, wondering what he was doing strolling through the park. When he'd looked up, his gaze landing unerringly on her, she'd felt raw and exposed. Though she'd stepped back immediately, it was as if she could still feel the weight of his gaze upon her.

Her stomach flipped, and for once it wasn't nausea; it was nerves. She was all but trembling at the prospect of facing him. Easing down onto the settee that rested beneath that window, she let out a deep, shaking breath that she hadn't even been aware she was holding. She wished Sabine were present, but she was resting in her own home, and given how much the woman had done for her in the past week, it was well-deserved rest.

Sabine had found a midwife who'd provided a miraculous tonic for her that relieved all but the worst of her nausea. The mornings were still truly wretched, but at least by afternoon she could climb out of bed and manage to eat toast and drink tea—and keep it down.

Reaching for the sewing basket on the floor beside her, she retrieved it and set to work. Busy hands always soothed a worried mind. It was the best way to await his arrival.

She couldn't say how long it took before a soft knock sounded on her door. It wasn't Sinclair. It was her maid.

"His lordship is in the drawing room, my lady. He asked that I relay an invitation to join him."

"Tell him I'll be there directly, please," she answered.

Sarah nodded and then slipped out.

Rising from the settee, she smoothed her gown. At

least the high-waisted style hid her growing belly. It wouldn't be entirely obvious the moment she walked through the door. Though she did not doubt that he was already aware of her condition. Gray would have told him and likely scolded him on her behalf. But no one had scolded her, and she'd behaved horribly. Sabine had been firm but kind and understanding. *Much more so than I deserved*, she thought with intense regret. How much misery had she caused by simply not being able to believe him—to believe *in* him?

With another deep breath and a pat of her hair, she left her room, sewing box in hand, and made for the stairs. When she reached the bottom, she turned and walked into the drawing room, with no notion of what to expect.

He was standing before the fireplace, a cheery fire blazing inside it. His back was to her, and she could see that he desperately needed a haircut. The sandy-blond locks were far longer than she'd ever seen them before, well past his shirt collar and resting on his shoulders. Immediately, her fingers twitched, itching to touch him, to feel those silken strands gliding though them. Then he turned to face her, and she realized just how awful he looked—his face gaunt, eyes hollow, and complexion paler than she'd ever known him to be.

She gasped. "You look positively wretched!"

His lips quirked in that sarcastic half smile she knew so intimately. "I've no doubt of it. And while the sight of you is a balm to me, you do not look well, Thea. You do not look well. Not at all."

She laughed softly. "I am not well. Not at all. Though I am better than I was a week past. And you? Are you better?"

"I am better now. I am better with you," he said softly.

Her heart stuttered in her chest. "You don't need to say those things. Not to me. I understand this is not what you wanted. Not what you planned. Lady Bruxton—"

"Can hang," he interjected. "She can bloody well hang. She's a vicious, lying cat, and I should never have underestimated her. I will say this one time only, Thea: I do not want Charlotte. Independent of whatever happens between us, I will never be with Charlotte. Anything she might have said to the contrary was either fiction or fantasy on her part."

She tried to speak, but for the longest time it seemed she was just opening and closing her mouth, with no sound emerging. Finally, she managed, "You mean that. You really do!"

"I do. And I'm sorry I ever gave you cause to doubt it."

"But you didn't," she protested. "All of those doubts, Sinclair...they were my own. They did not come from you. For years, all I heard from my father, on a daily basis, was how ugly and stupid I was, that I was plain and unattractive and lazy and that no man would ever want me for a wife. Though I knew him to be a liar, though I knew him to be vicious and cruel for the sake of it, when you hear something often enough, you believe it. And I did. I believed him, and I kept waiting for you to grow bored and disinterested, because how could you not? You were everything, and I was nothing."

"Do not ever say that, that you were nothing. You were bright and funny. You were kind and giving. You were also occasionally contrary, argumentative, and maddening. And I love you, Thea, for all those reasons and more. For everything that you are, I love you. I should have swallowed my damned pride and said it so often you'd have laughed in the face of Charlotte's machinations because you would never have a moment to doubt my feelings for you."

The enormity of what he'd just said swamped her. It was like going under water. She couldn't catch her breath. And then the tears came, great, gulping sobs that wracked her until she could do nothing but tremble and weep.

"Thea... Althea," he said. "What is wrong? If you do not feel that way—"

"I've loved you for years," she admitted tearfully. "Even when I didn't even know you. I'd see you in the village, and you would take my breath away. You never looked twice in my direction, and I never dared to dream that it would ever be anything more than just an unrequited infatuation. And when I met you, you were not at all the perfect gentleman I had imagined. You were not charming or even especially genteel in your manner toward me, and I thought all my days pining for you had been a bitter waste. But I could not have been more wrong. You are not perfect, but I do not need you to be perfect, Sinclair. I only need you to be you, and I need to be yours. That is all I will ever need. And I will never be foolish enough to let my stubborn pride or the doubts from my past get in the way of that again."

"I want to restore Rosedale Manor," he said. "I want to make it a home for us...unless you've no wish to live there. I know Boston Spa has not been a kind place to you."

"It's my home. It's your home. And I'd love to see it restored. The house should not suffer for what others did."

"Treason," he admitted. "My father and my grandfather were well paid... The original manor was Tudor—old and dark. It did not fit my grandfather's aesthetic. He wished to make it bright and palatial. He wanted something so grand that he would be the envy of others. So, he and my father sold secrets to our enemies: the colonials, the French...whoever would pay their price. But Rosedale stood long before their sins, and it should stand after, stripped of what they did to it."

"And to you. Their shame isn't yours, Sinclair. It never was."

He looked away, clearly not quite ready to part with his guilt over that. "There are things I cannot make amends for, but it doesn't change the fact that an indeterminate part of my fortune comes from their misdeeds. I support charities for widows and orphans of the wars. I've funded housing and hospitals for wounded soldiers. But I cannot make it right."

"It doesn't have to be right. Only better," she offered. "And I'll help you. We'll make it better together."

"I love you, Thea. And I'll never make you unhappy again."

"I love you," she answered in return. "And I'll never let you. I'll be contrary, maddening and difficult, to remind you of all the reasons you love me."

He stepped forward, and before she could even fathom what he meant to do, he swept her up into his arms, kissing her soundly.

Oh, she had missed that. The feel of him against her, the taste of his lips, the rasp of his shadowy whiskers on her skin. Could anything be more perfect? And then he was moving them to the larger settee, bearing her back against the cushions as that kiss turned to something else. It was no longer simply about rejoicing in their reconciliation. The familiar heat bloomed between them, and the need that she had thought would never again be fulfilled roared to life inside her.

"We should go upstairs," she suggested. "This is scandalous in the drawing room."

"I've spent the last week on horseback, Thea. If I have to climb those stairs again, we won't be able to do this," he admitted. "Scandal be damned."

She laughed. "Then, by all means, yes. Scandal be damned."

COMING SOON: THE PERFECT GROOM

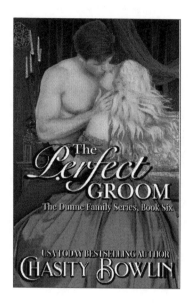

Miss Penelope Dennings grew a conscience and made an enemy. By confessing her role in the events that nearly destroyed the marriage of Lord and Lady Mayville, she helped to bring them back together... but it has cost her everything. Her friends have turned their backs on her and she is all but a pariah in society.

Theo Blake, Lord Ralston, is a man who needs a wife. Any wife. His title and entailed estates are secure, but a significant inheritance hangs in the balance if he remains a bachelor. There's only one problem. He's too nice. Handsome and even rich, when compared to the rogues, rakes and general bad boys of society, there is really no comparison. All the eligible ladies simply look over him as if he were completely invisible.

But invisibility gives him a unique insight into Miss Dennings terrible situation. So Ralston makes her an offer—one she cannot refuse. But not everyone wants to see them settled in a happy union. Jealousy is an ugly and destructive force and Theo, for the first time in his life, might have to fight dirty to get what he wants. And despite the rather perfunctory nature of their courtship, he's realized that what he wants, above all else, is Penelope...

EPILOGUE

One Year Later

ALTHEA HEARD the carriage wheels before she rounded the corner of the house. The small garden had become her sanctuary, as the house was forever under construction. But she wouldn't complain. Stripping away the artifice of Rosedale Manor and returning the house to its Tudor origins had given Sinclair purpose, and Sinclair with a purpose was a magnificent thing indeed. The ennui and sarcasm that had reflected how deeply unhappy he'd been were simply gone. In their place was a man who was excited to begin each day.

A soft mewling sound drew her gaze, and she stared down at the small bundle in her arms. Their son, Grayson Sinclair Wortham, had been born at Rosedale Manor, the place he would call home. While the first six months of her pregnancy had been a misery, the last three had seen her glowing with health and vitality. Even the delivery had been shockingly quick and easy. But she would not take that for granted.

Patting the baby soothingly, she continued toward the front of the house, just as the carriage halted. The doors sprung open, and Sabine was out of the carriage and running towards her.

"Oh, let me see him! I know he's grown so much," Sabine cried out.

Untying the shawl which she used to support her son's not insubstantial weight, she relinquished him into Sabine's waiting arms. "He has a very healthy appetite."

"My goodness, he certainly does! Are you well? Truly?"

Althea smiled. "I could not be better. Only heaven could be better than this. Even then, I would take some convincing."

Sabine laughed at that just as Sinclair emerged from the house. He smiled at them but did not interrupt their talk. Instead, he headed straight for Gray, and the two men began conversing about the renovations.

"He certainly looks well," Sabine observed.

"He is. Remarkably so. Fatherhood and home renovations seem to suit him tremendously well."

"I wonder if fatherhood will suit Gray so perfectly?"

There was a note in Sabine's tone, one of pure giddiness and joy, that told the truth of it even before she asked the question. "Are you with child?"

"I am. And much farther along this time than last. Nearly five months gone," she admitted. "Gray knows, and now you, but we've told no one else. I was afraid to hope, but the midwife—the one who attended you in Bath—she has helped me. I've been taking these vile-tasting herbal teas she has given me. They're awful, but I'll drink them by the barrel if need be."

"Let's go to the garden and have our tea there. It is a beautiful day, after all. But they will all be beautiful to you from now on, won't they?"

"WHAT DO you think they're whispering about?" Mayville asked.

"They're likely trying to plan a wedding between my daughter and your son."

Mayville grinned. "How do you know it will be a daughter?"

"I don't, really. I want it to be. Is that strange? I'd rather have a miniature version of my lovely wife to spoil than an heir," Gray mused.

"I don't think it's strange," Mayville answered. "I hope we are blessed with one, as well. Though Thea says she hopes any daughter we have should look like me. She insists I am the prettier of us."

"I wouldn't go that far." Gray shuddered. "But you are ridiculously pretty. It's unseemly for a man. Oh, and it will never happen, by the way."

"My daughter won't look like me?"

"My daughter will never marry your son. She'll never marry anyone's son. She will remain sweet, innocent and free from all the wretched misery that men bring to women in this world," Gray stated flatly. "So don't let him get any ideas."

"I do not let him do anything." Mayville laughed. "I cannot wait for you to discover just how little control you will actually have. That, my friend, will be the second greatest joy of my life!"

At that moment, Sabine and Althea laughed. Gray shrugged. "I'd asked what the first was, but I'm not a fool. She makes you happy."

"She is my heart, and that very loud bundle your wife is staring at adoringly is my soul. The very best of me is in him," Mayville said. "As it should be."

"As it should be," Gray concurred. "Now, let's go and stop them before they have the banns posted."

YOU CAN PREORDER THE NEXT BOOK IN THE DUNNE SERIES BY CLICKING HERE

ALSO BY CHASITY BOWLIN

THE DARK REGENCY SERIES

The Haunting of a Duke

The Redemption of a Rogue

The Enticement of an Earl

A Love So Dark

A Passion So Strong

A Heart So Wicked

An Affair So Destined

STANDALONE

The Beast of Bath

Worth The Wait

THE DUNNE FAMILY SERIES

The Last Offer

The First Proposal

The Other Wife

The Late Husband

The Plain Bride (coming soon)

The Perfect Groom (coming soon)

THE LOST LORDS SERIES

The Lost Lord of Castle Black

The Vanishing of Lord Vale

The Missing Marquess of Althorn

The Resurrection of Lady

The Mystery of Miss Mason

The Awakening of Lord Ambrose

Hyacinth

A Midnight Clear

The Pirate's Bluestocking (A Pirates of Britannia Crossover)

THE VICTORIAN GOTHIC COLLECTION

House of Shadows

Veil of Shadows

Passage of Shadows

THE HELLION CLUB SERIES

A Rogue to Remember

Barefoot in Hyde Park

What Happens In Piccadilly

Sleepless In Southampton

When An Earl Loves A Governess (coming soon)

The Duke's Magnificent Obsession

The Governess Diaries

THE LYON'S DEN CONNECTED WORLD

Fall Of The Lyon

Tamed By The Lyon

THE WYLDE WALLFLOWERS

One Wylde Night

A Kiss Gone Wylde (coming soon)

Too Wylde To Tame (coming soon)

Wylde At Heart (coming soon)

Made in United States
Orlando, FL
08 July 2024

48733280R00121